Looking for the

Lost Gods of England

Kathleen Herbert

Anglo-Saxon Books

First Published 1994
Reprinted 1995/1998/2000/2/5/7/10

Published by
Anglo-Saxon Books
www.asbooks.co.uk
Hereward, Black Bank Road, Little Downham
Ely, Cambridgeshire CB6 2UA England

Printed by Lightning Source
Australia, England, USA

PL

British Library Cataloguing-in-Publication Data. A catalogue record
for this book is available from the British Library.

ISBN 9781898281610

Contents

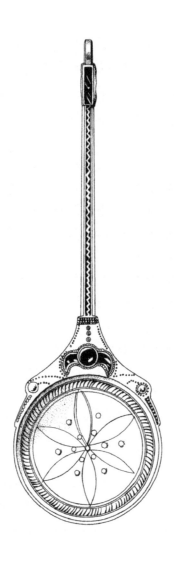

Anglo-Saxon strainer from a heathen period grave

Drawn by Lindsay Kerr

Foreword

Kathleen Herbert read English at Oxford where she heard Tolkien's lectures; as a result she has been working with Old English literature and early English culture ever since. She is particularly interested in the relationship between history and the creative imagination, and has explored this in lectures and articles, also in historical novels and short stories.

The following text is a transcript of a talk given by Kathleen Herbert to a meeting of Þa Engliscan Gesiþas (The English Companions). The first three maps and other information at the back of the book are based on the handouts provided by Kathleen for those attending the meeting. The publisher has added the last two maps.

Details of Þa Engliscan Gesiþas can be found at the back of this book.

Anglo-Saxon brooches and beads

Drawn by Lindsay Kerr

Looking for the Lost Gods of England

In the year 597, Hengest's great-grandson, King Æðelbert of Kent, met a group of priests who had come with a message for him from Pope Gregory in Rome. The king insisted on meeting them in the open air, which would blow away any spells they might try to cast on him with their alien magic. But this magic was too strong to be blown away on the wind. Less than a century later, all the English kingdoms were officially Christian.

So the beliefs and traditions of the earlier faith lost most of their royal and scholarly patronage. Therefore there was no powerful motive for recording them. However, there were three very important exceptions to this neglect in high places.

The royal genealogies still claimed one or another of the old gods as the divine ancestor of the royal dynasties. A true king had to be god-born. In most of the genealogies, the first-father is Woden. As early as the first century, the Romans had noted that the Germanic tribes paid special reverence to "Mercurius"[1]; they were under the impression that he was the only god who received human sacrifice.

The second place to look for traces of the old religion is in the Old English medical and other educational works.[2] Items of pre-Christian learning were

---

[1] Tacitus: *Germania* ch. 9. The text, with parallel English translation, is in *Tacitus vol. I*, Loeb Classical Library no. 35.

[2] The magico-medical texts are available in modern translation and with much commentary and additional information in *Leechcraft: Early English Charms, Plantlore and Healing*; Stephen Pollington, Anglo-Saxon Books, 2003.
The magico-medical texts were edited for the Rolls Series by T. O. Cockayne as *Leechdoms, Wortcunning and Starcraft of Early England*, 3 vols. 1864–66; reprint 1965.
Bede's work on the computation of time contains observations on early English seasonal rites: *Bedae Opera De Temporibus* ed. C. W. Jones, Cambridge (Mass.) 1943.
More general discussion of the subjects can be found in:
Anglo-Saxon Magic G. Storms 1948
cont. next page

recorded, copied and preserved in Christian manuscripts because the prescriptions worked and the information was still useful. For example, Bede's account of the old English names of the months takes us through the course of a pagan English farmer's year. Bede, of course, had no intention of giving us a liturgical calendar of heathen English rites and says as little as possible about them; he was writing a treatise on the calculation of dates for Christian movable feasts. However, *De Temporum Ratione*, together with the leechbooks and some anecdotes in chronicles and biographies, gives some vivid glimpses of the old faith in action.

The third refuge of early tradition is the Old English courtly and heroic poetry; that is where most modern readers first meet it. Unluckily, in 1066, English poetry also lost its royal and most – not all – of its wealthy and scholarly patronage for over two hundred years to come.

The loss of official status means that there is no neat, formalised account of the old English religion and its rites, with each supernatural power clearly defined, such as is found in Classical and Norse mythology. What is left of Old England has survived without such help, through its vitality, because it is an expression of some part of the English psyche. The material is fascinating; some of it is very beautiful but it is not easy to summarise. To find it, we have to search through museums, Old English poetry, Old English magic, medieval ballads and popular songs, collections of local folklore. To make sense of it, we have to look beyond England, to the Northern Bronze Age, to Roman accounts of the early Germans, to medieval accounts of old Norse mythology and religious practices – and then argue fiercely about the relevance of such comparisons.

The first thing to bear in mind is that the country now called England is, in fact, our second England, New England. The first England – Old Anglia, Engla land, Angeln – was in the south of the country we now call Denmark. Angeln was in the narrow neck of the Cimbric peninsula, with the River Eider as its southern frontier. This frontier was defended and fixed by King Offa I, in one of the great exploits of early English tradition, a tale of self-penalising honour that is very nearly a thousand years older than the medieval Age of Chivalry.

Anglo-Saxon Magic and Medicine (illustrated specially from the semi-pagan text *Lacnunga*) J. H. G. Grattan & C. Singer 1952.

Therefore, during our formative period of at least two thousand years, the centre of our world was a good way further to the east, so our world-view was very different from that of today.

To the north of the peninsula were the Jutes; nearby and in the islands were the other five tribes who were allied with the English in a religious confederacy. The Danes were in the southernmost tip of modern Sweden, Skåne (the Scandza of Jordanes; the Scedeland of *Beowulf*, I.19). Beyond them, south of the great lakes, in Väster- and Öster-götland, were the Geats, Beowulf's people. The Swedes were north of the lakes, with their great religious centre at Uppsala.

North of the Swedes, and also in Finland, were the people then called Finns, whom we know as Lapps. The north Germanic tribes held them in awe as the greatest masters of magic in the human race. The Old English metrical charms show that the early English used shamanastic techniques in their medical practice: healers would engage in spirit-combats with the spirits of the attacking infections and ailments.

South of the peninsula, in the lands around the lower Elbe and Weser, were the Suebic tribes. The first Roman writer to mention the English makes no reference to Saxons. Like Franks, it is the name of a later confederation of tribes from this area. The Saxons were of Suebic stock; their earlier English neighbours called them *Swæfe*; later they were known as Old Saxons, to distinguish them from the folk who had crossed to Britain.

According to the ancient Germanic legend of origins, that was preserved in the ancient hymns which were their only kind of record and history – *"carminibus antiquis, quod unum apud illos memoriae et annalium genus est"*[3] – the tribes nearest the ocean, in the Cimbric peninsula and in Baltic Scandinavia, were the Ingaevones, the descendants of Ing, the Son of Mannus.

At the eastern end of the Baltic lived the Æstii. They were not the people we know as Estonians, who are a Finno-Ugric race. The Æstii were Indo-European Balts; their language was probably the ancestor of Old Prussian, similar to Lithuanian. In early times, when neighbouring branches from the same linguistic root had not grown so far apart, the Æstii could share their ideas with their East Germanic kin.

---

[3] *Germania* ch. 3.

No one knows exactly when the Goths and Burgundians set out from Gotland and Bornholm on the long trek that was to take some of them to the Black Sea, and to rulership in Italy, Spain and Gaul. In the course of their remarkable and tragic adventures, they added many heroic and romantic tales to the Germanic store.

The world, as the early Germans knew it, offered vast scope for adventure and rich food for the imagination, from the wastes of Lappland to the dazzling splendours of Constantinople and Rome; from the eastern steppes, where the Gothic horsemen came up against the Iranian Sarmatians and Alans and the Turkic Huns, to the western "country-house" life in the villas of Gaul and Spain.

The English did not leave that world behind when they crossed the sea and founded their new England. They brought their stories with them and went on re-creating them in their poetry. Only a fragment of Old English poetry remains: one epic only survives as two scraps that were later used in book-binding.

However, the heroes and stories of all the main Germanic nations, except the Vandals, are referred to in the fragments that we have. The Vandals seem to have vanished from the English mental map when they crossed to Africa, where they were wiped off the political map by Belisarius. Remembering the mainland and the Heroic Age, the poets ranged in imagination, westwards with the Visigoth Waldere and his gallant lady fighting their way back to Aquitaine; eastwards to Eormanric's warriors meeting the onslaught of the Huns –

"Þonne Hræda here heardum sweordum
ymb Wistlawudu wergan sceoldon
ealdne eþelstol Ætlan leodum"

– when the Gothic war-host had to defend their ancient homeland with their hard swords against Attila's folk in the forest of the Vistula.[4]

---

[4] *Widsið*, ll 120–22. Text in A.S.P.R. vol. III *The Exeter Book* ed. G. P. Krapp & E. v K. Dobbie, Columbia U.P. 1936.
The edition by R. W. Chambers: *Widsið, A study in Old English Heroic legend* C.U.P. 1912 has a commentary that provides a "Who was Who in the Heroic Age of Germania".

English poets and their listeners seem to have been stirred most (judging by the remaining material; but surviving by luck and chance, this may not be completely representative) by the stories which had grown up around their own Baltic and North Sea coasts: Offa's defence of the English border and his winning of a perilous maiden; the self-destruction of the Scylding House; the exploits of Beowulf; Hengest's bitter choices; the agony of Weland; the doomed enchantment of Heoden's love for Hild.

The English were a Baltic people. The Romans said that they had remained undisturbed and inaccessible by enemies *"fluminibus aut silviis muniuntur"*, fortified with rivers and forests.[5] Archaeology confirms that there was no invasion of peoples or cultures from the outside, during a period from the beginning of the Northern Bronze Age (c. 1500 BCE) to the Migrations of the third century CE onwards.

This means that the people who called themselves *Engle* (written as *Anglii* in Latin) were forming their group-identity during the brilliant Bronze Age culture of the Cimbric peninsula, that has left such spectacular and mind-teasing remains: the curved ceremonial trumpets, the *lurs*; the ritual horned helmets; the fine metal-work of weapons, collars and drinking-horns; the figurines of girls in the briefest of cord mini-skirts (they really did wear them; the garments have been found in burials); above all, the carved rock-pictures.[6]

These images seem to be concerned with evoking and celebrating fertility. Such images have been used worldwide for this purpose: the tree; the horned animal; the man with the erect penis; the pairing of man and woman; the acrobatic leaps that symbolise energy and growth. Particularly significant in relation to later English practices are the *ship*, slim and light in build; the *waggon* or *wain*; the *plough* and above all the *sun*, represented as a disc with crossing spokes, which is often being used as a *shield* by the stick-like male figures.

---

5 *Germania* ch. 40.

6 For the rock-pictures see *the Chariot of the Sun* P. Gelling with
H. E. Davidson 1969.   For pre-historic Denmark see *Land of the Tollund Man*
P. Lauring trans. R. Spink 1957
There is a good selection of illustrations in *Scandinavian Mythology*
H. E. Davidson 1982 but the reader must note the place and date of the finds to
see which material is relevant to the *Anglii* and their allies.

In Old English and other Germanic languages the sun is feminine: in the north, she is gentle, life-giving, nurturing; she does not burn the earth or strike folk to death.

The earliest surviving mention of the English as a separate tribe comes in the *Germania* of Tacitus, published in 98 CE. Tacitus describes German society of the first century as being of the 'heroic' type, which existed at different periods, and with regional variations, among the Indo-European peoples from India to Ireland. The leading characters in these societies are the kings and chiefs and their 'companions', élite warriors bound to their lords by ties of honour, courage and generosity.

Tacitus mentions three great gods by more or less equivalent Latin names: Mars, Mercury and Hercules; later the Romans corrected the last name to Jupiter. These gods were known in Old English as Tiw, Woden and Thunor, who are still commemorated in the weekday names Tuesday *Tiwes dæg*, Wednesday *Wodnes dæg* and Thursday *Þunres dæg*. When English scholars learned to read and write in Latin, they accepted these Roman names as reasonably accurate translations. Tacitus stresses that the Germans believed there was something specially holy about woman as a sex, "*sanctum aliquid*"[7]; that they had special prophetic powers; that men consulted them and followed their advice on matters of politics and war.

The English seem to have conformed to the general Germanic pattern, because Tacitus says that there was nothing noteworthy about them and the six tribes who shared in their worship *except one thing*. However, he found that one exception so interesting and important that he gave it a whole chapter in a very short book:

> "They worship in common Nerthus, that is Terra Mater [Earth Mother] and believe she intervenes in human affairs and goes on progress through the tribes. There is a sacred grove on an island of the ocean, and in the grove is a consecrated waggon [or wain] covered with a cloth [possibly embroidered or woven with golden thread, like the scraps found in the Taplow burial]. Only one priest is allowed to touch it; he understands when the goddess is present in her shrine and follows with profound reverence when she is drawn away by cows [*bubus feminis*]. Then there are days of rejoicing: the places she considers worthy to

---

[7] *Germania* ch. 8.

entertain her – [that is, wherever the cows drawing the wain, which has no human driver, come to a stop] – keep holiday. They do not go to war, do not use weapons, all iron is shut away – peace and quiet are so much esteemed and loved at that time – until the same priest returns the goddess to her sanctuary when she has had enough of human company. Directly, the wain, the covering cloth and, if you like to believe this, [here Tacitus, the sophisticated Roman, distances himself from the English and their primitive beliefs] the goddess herself, are washed in a secluded lake. Slaves are the ministers; immediately, the same lake swallows them. [They are drowned as soon as they have finished their task; lay folk may not see or touch the goddess and live.] From this arises a mysterious terror and a pious ignorance about what that may be, which is only seen by those about to die."[8]

So, the noteworthy characteristic of the English, to foreign eyes, was that they were goddess-worshippers; they looked on the earth as their mother.

They did not leave this relationship behind them when they crossed over to another part of the earth; not even when they had crossed over to another state religion. Among the Old English healers' prescriptions, which in their surviving forms were written down in the tenth and eleventh centuries, is one named *Æcerbot*: Field-Remedy.[9] It is called a 'charm'; in fact, it is a full-scale ritual which would take a whole day to perform, as well as the time needed to collect and prepare all the materials that it calls for.

As we have it, the ritual has been extensively Christianised. It not only entails much reciting of Latin liturgical texts by the healer, but it needs four masses, to be said over four turfs that are taken to church and placed with their grassy sides facing the altar. These turfs represent the sick field. This could only happen with the approval and co-operation of the parish priest. Four masses could take up most of a morning; there is no way that the priest could be unaware – or even pretend to be unaware – what was going on. And what was going on, after her healing, was a mating of Mother Earth with the God of Heaven and her impregnation by Him.

---

[8] *Germania* ch. 40.

[9] See Rodrigues and Cockayne, works cited in footnote 2 above. There is a translation in *Anglo-Saxon Poetry* S. A. J. Bradley 1982.

Leaving out the recitation of Latin texts, what happened was this: Mother Earth, in this particular field, was weak and sick, unable to bear. Perhaps she had been deliberately injured by hostile magic.

The healer cut a turf from each of the four quarters: east, south, west and north, noting carefully exactly where each had lain. These turfs for the time being represented –were the whole field. A mixture was made of vegetable matter from every tree and shrub that grew locally, except hardwoods, and all known herbs except buckbean. These were blended with oil, honey, holy water and milk from all the cattle on the farm. This mixture was dropped three times on the underside of the turfs.

Mother Earth was being given healing herbs, mixed with a nourishing porridge to strengthen her.

Then the turfs went to church for their four masses. Presumably these replaced something that was once done in a temple or a sacred grove. They were put back exactly where they came from, but first, four crosses made of 'quickbeam' – the name was used later for both the rowan and the wild service tree – with the names of the evangelists cut on their ends, were placed in the earth under them.

In the light of what follows, these crosses may originally have been the spokes of the sun-wheel, with *sigel* ᛋ and other appropriate runes cut in them, but this is only guess-work.

The healer faced eastwards, praying to "*þone haligan heofonrices weard ...and heofones meaht and heah reced,*" the holy guardian of the heavenly kingdom ...and the might of heaven and the high hall; then turned three times with the course of the sun and fell prostrate on the earth.

The warmth and life-giving power of the sun was now pouring down through the body of the healer on to and into Mother Earth.

Then the plough was got ready. A hole was drilled into the plough beam and another mixture was put into it: incense, fennel and consecrated salt, blended with consecrated salve. (*Sape* means 'salve', 'unguent', or 'soap' in Old English.) Had the priest blessed the ointment, whatever it was – or did he let them use the oil for anointing the sick?

After the anointing, seed specially bought from beggars at double the value was placed on the body of the plough. The plough, which figures in the Bronze Age rock pictures, is a traditional symbol for the penis. Shakespeare describes Cleopatra's seduction of Julius Caesar as:

"She made great Caesar lay his sword to bed,
he ploughed her and she cropped..."

which is exactly what this ritual was designed to bring about. Before the plough/penis was put into Mother Earth, it had to be anointed and made potent with semen.

The healer then recited a prayer that the earth might be granted a bountiful harvest and be kept safe from all harm "from witchcrafts (or poisons) sown across the land". The opening line of this prayer is mysterious: *"Erce, erce, erce, eorþan modor* –Erce, erce, erce, Mother of Earth", with its three-fold and untranslated invocation and the fact that the power being addressed is not Mother Earth but the Mother of Earth, whoever she may be.

Then the plough was set in motion and the first furrow was cut as the marriage-blessing was recited:

"Hal wes þu, folde, fira modor,
beo þu growende on Godes fæðme,
fodre gefylled firum to nytte

Hail to you, earth, mother of mortals, may you grow big in God's embrace, filled with food for the use of humankind."

Mother Earth was being penetrated and impregnated, but one wonders which god was supposed to be doing it. At the time this ritual was written down, the official answer should have been Jehovah, but this is not easy to visualise.

Then the healer, or the assistants, took flour made from every kind of grain, kneaded with milk and holy water. A loaf or cake was baked, as big as would fit into a pair of hollowed palms, and put inside the first furrow with another blessing. Mother Earth has got a corn-baby.

So, as the count of years was adding up to 1,000 of the Christian era, the English were still in the service of Nerthus. They went on serving her through all the upheavals of history for the next thousand years, Before looking at later examples of her rites, it will be helpful to study her corn-baby more closely.

After the first Danish war, King Alfred organised a massive literary and educational programme. One of the items to be re-organised was the royal genealogy. The royal House of Wessex, soon to become what it still is, the royal House of all England, was at that time the champion of Christendom against the heathen Vikings. Yet the first ancestor of the dynasty was Woden. That did not bother them in the least; they were happy to go on naming Woden among their ancestors. What worried them was that they could not count so many generations as the House of David and Judah, so their line did not reach back to Adam. Their scholars and scops quickly set that right by adding in the requisite number of legendary heroes from the Old English poetry and tradition.[10] The three highest names on the new list, which take it up to Noah, where it merges with the pedigree in *Genesis*, are:

> Scef *Sheaf, "who was born in Noah's ark",*
> Scyld *Shield, his son,*
> Beow *Barley, his son. This is the being, later known as John Barleycorn, whose passion, death and resurrection are told in a folk song, which also celebrates the reviving effects of drinking his blood.*

These new forefathers must have been approved by the royal house. Perhaps their names were suggested by one of its members, who might have been King Alfred himself. Around 990, a nobleman of royal descent, the Ealdorman Æðelweard, added this note to the genealogy:

> "This Sheaf came to land in a light boat, surrounded by weapons, on an island in the ocean which is called Scani. [The southern tip of Sweden, the ancient home of the Danes.] He was indeed a very young child and

---

[10] Two versions of the longer West Saxon genealogy (one in the Parker Chronicle, the other in the Abingdon Chronicles) are given under the year 855: see *the Anglo-Saxon Chronicle* pp. 66–7, trans. and ed. G. N. Garmonsway, Dent pbk. no. 1624.

The Chronicle of Æðelweard (trans. and ed. by A. Campbell, Nelson's Medieval Texts 1962) takes the line up to Beo, Scyld and Scef; he adds the following note: "Ipse Scef cum uno dromone advectus est in insula oceani, quae dicitur Scani, armis circumdatus, eratque valde recens puer, et ab incolis illius terrae ignotus; attamen ab eis suscipitur et ut familiarem diligenti animo eum custodierunt et post in regem eligunt; de cuius prosapia ordinem trahit Athulf rex." (King Æðelwulf)

Æðelweard was the great-great-grandson of King Æðelræd, elder brother of Alfred the Great. He was a layman, ealdorman of "the western provinces" Dorset, Somerset and Devon. He wrote his chronicle for his cousin Matilda. She was the great-great-granddaughter of Alfred, through the marriage of his granddaughter Eadgyð to Otto the Great. Though this chronicle is not a masterpiece of Latin historical writing, it does show the literacy of the West Saxon royal family and their continuing interest in their Germanic connections.

unknown to the folk of that land. However, they took him up and looked after him as carefully as if he were one of their own kin and afterwards elected him king. And King Æðelwulf [father of Alfred the Great] came from the line of his descendants."

Danish traditions about their legendary history and the origins of their royal house make no mention of this story.

About 150 years after Æðelweard's note, the English historian William of Malmesbury retold the story of Sheaf with some extra details:

"He was brought as a child in a ship without oars... he was asleep and a sheaf of corn lay at his head. Therefore he was called Sheaf and taken for a miracle by the people of that region and carefully fostered. When he grew up, he reigned in a town that was then called Slaswic and now called Haithebi (Hedeby). Now that district is called Old Anglia... from it the Anglii came to Britain."[11]

The Old English patronymic was '*ing*', used as a suffix. In the Wessex genealogy, Shield son of Sheaf would be Scyld Scefing; Barley, son of Shield would be Beow Scylding. Readers of *Beowulf* meet Scyld Scefing at the beginning of the poem; he is the wonder-child who comes "ænne ofer yðe, alone over the waves" to become the ancestor of the Danish royal dynasty and whose corpse departs into the unknown, probably in the same otherworldly ship that brought him, with a cargo of priceless treasures.

This version of the story is also unknown to the Danes. Their royal dynasty was called the Scyldings, and it took its name from Scyld. This Scyld, however, was not an unknown foundling who came from overseas; he was the grandson of their eponymous ancestor Dan – the 'Dane', who had a younger brother called 'Angul'.

---

[11] *De Gestis Regum Anglorum* Bk II (ed. W. Stubbs, Rolls Series 1887–9)
"Iste, ut ferunt, in quandam insulam Germaniae Scandzam, de qua Jordanes, historiographus Gothorum, loquitur, appulsus navi sine remige, puerulus, posito ad caput frumenti manipulo, dormiens, ideoque Sceaf nuncupatus, ab hominibus regionis illius pro miraculo exceptus et sedulo nutritus: adulta aetate regnavit in oppido quod tunc Slaswic, nunc vero Haithebi appellatur. Est autem regio illa Anglia vetus dicta . . . "
There is detailed discussion of the royal genealogies, also of the references to Scyld and Scef in *Beowulf, an Introduction to the Study of the Poem* R. W. Chambers, 3rd ed. with supplement by C. L. Wren 1963.

On the other hand, the legend of the saviour-king's arrival and departure over the waves seems to have deep roots in the English consciousness.

"From the great deep to the great deep he goes."

Tennyson inserted the story of the arrival of the wonder-child in a dragon-ship into the Arthurian legend, where it has no place.[12] In 1939 when the shape of a vanished ship was found in a burial mound at Sutton Hoo, still carrying a cargo of priceless treasures, the opening lines of *Beowulf* were expounded to the coroner's jury, to help them decide whether the cargo was treasure trove.

Looking at the sequence: Sheaf, Shield, Barley, in the Wessex genealogy, it is easy to see why the barleycorn sown at the New Year ploughing should be seen as the off-spring of last year's harvested sheaf – but why did a shield come between?

In the reign of King Edmund I (941–946), the monks of the Abbey of Abingdon were in dispute about possession of some meadows bordering on the Thames downstream. The monks used what seems to us a very strange way of proving that the Abbey owned the land, though they set it down in their chronicle as a matter of course:

> Appealing to the judgement of God, the monks put a sheaf of corn, with a lighted taper at its head, onto a round shield and launched the shield into the Thames where it flowed past the abbey. The shield floated down towards the disputed ground, followed by a few monks in a small boat. The shield was carried towards one bank or the other, depending on which side the abbey estates happened to be. [Thus proving that whatever power was steering the shield knew which land belonged to the abbey.] Then the shield came to the mouth of a little tributary bordering the lands the abbey claimed. Because of heavy and prolonged rainfall, the Thames was flowing high and strong, forcing a way into the mouth of the stream, so that its own waters had flooded the land behind. This floodwater was making its way into the Thames lower down, so that the disputed meadows were now an island. The current

---

[12] *The Coming of Arthur* I.410 (in *Idylls of the King*, ed. J. M. Gray, Penguin English Poets 1983. It is interesting to compare ll.20–31 and 358–410 in this poem with the stories of Scef quoted above and with the arrival of Scyld in *Beowulf* ll.4–8 and 43–47.

swept the shield, with its sheaf and taper, up the tributary, across the flooded land and back into the Thames, having circumnavigated the area that the abbey claimed so proving – apparently to everyone's satisfaction – that the abbey's claim was just.[13]

The monks deserve credit for having made a careful study of the Thames currents and the movements of the floodwater. Perhaps they had made a trial voyage over the course; but what, or who, did they think was giving the verdict in their favour? A shield with a sheaf on it – Scyld Scefing (the words will bear that sense) – or a sheaf travelling in a shield as in a boat, bringing the secrets and gifts of Mother Earth to her human children, Sheaf the miracle child of Nerthus, now set in the monastic chronicles as the ancestor of their royal house?

In the Bronze Age pictures, the sun-discs are used as shields by the stick-like male figures. They are also placed with the ritual boats. The sun is needed to bring the crops. The story of the wonder-child from overseas contains some lost myth or ritual. If this was originally a celebration of the coming of agriculture to the north, with the miraculous enrichment that this must have brought to human life, then it could go back as far as 2500 BCE, which is about the time when this knowledge and skill developed in the Old Anglia.

The Abingdon divination rite must have developed among people to whom the sheaf was holy, full of godhead. In England we can find examples of the veneration of the sheaf, and the goddess who gave birth to the sheaf, continuing until the mechanisation and industrialisation of farming destroyed most of the old rituals.

On September 14th, 1598, a party of German visitors was going towards Eton. One of them wrote a description of the quaint behaviour of the natives:

> "We were returning to our lodging-house; by lucky chance we fell in with the country-folk celebrating their harvest-home. The last sheaf had been crowned with flowers and they had attached it to a magnificently robed image, *which perhaps they meant to represent Ceres*. [The Roman name for the goddess of the fruitful earth, especially the corn-harvest.] They carried her hither and thither with

---

[13] *Chronicon Monasterii de Abingdon* ed. Stevenson, Rolls Series 1858.

much noise; men and women were sitting together on the waggon, men-servants and maid-servants shouting through the streets until they came to the barn."[14]

About 1,500 years after Tacitus described the Nerthus rite, already long established among the continental English, the insular English had a goddess of the fruitful earth still riding in a waggon, making a random progress amidst public rejoicing. Servant-ministers were in attendance, though in the September (*Haligmonaþ*) of 1598, they were on their way to a more cheerful and less final end to the ceremonies.

Sometimes the role of the goddess was taken by a human representative, as at Maytime. In the song *Greensleeves*, the wretched lover reproaches his cool and grasping mistress with a list of all the presents he has lavished on her without getting anything in return. One of them was a magnificent gown:

"Thy gown was of the grassy green
With sleeves of satin hanging by,
Which made thee be our Harvest Queen –
But yet thou would'st not love me."

At the end of the 18th century, the antiquarian William Hutchinson reported meeting the Harvest Queen in Northumberland:

"I have seen in some places an image apparelled in great finery, crowned with flowers, a sheaf of corn placed under her arm and a scythe in her hand, carried out of the village in the morning of the concluding reaping day, with music and much clamour of the reapers, into the field where it stands fixed on a pole all day, and when the reaping is done it is brought home in like manner. This they call the *Harvest Queen* and *it represents the Roman Ceres*"

---

[14] The account is quoted in England as seen by Foreigners in the Days of Elizabeth and James I ed. W. B. Rye 1865:
"Cum hic ad diversorium nostrum reverteremur, forte fortuna incidimus in rusticos spicilegia sua celebrantes, qui ultimam frugum vehem floribus conorant, addita imagine splendide vestita, qua Cererem forsitan significare volentes, eam hinc inde movent et magna cum clamore. Viri juxta et mulieres, servi atque ancillae, currui insidentes per plateas vociferantur, donec ad horreum deveniant."

To classically educated scholars from one end of Europe to the other, all the old gods appeared in their Roman forms. At least, they recognized that the Harvest Queen was a goddess, not a corn-dolly. Whatever she is called: Ceres, Harvest Queen, Earth Mother of mortals, Nerthus, she is the special goddess of the English.

It is one of the odd results of the conversion that the most complete overview of Old English seasonal rites should be found in works meant for teaching the *computus*, the complicated method of working out the dates of the movable feasts in the Christian year. The scholarly authors – Bede, Ælfric, Byrhtferð – had, of course, no desire to give detailed instructions about the heathen sacred year. They tell as little as possible about the native way of reckoning time, just enough to help English readers understand the Latin terms. They record enough, though, to show how closely the Old English sacred year was bound up with the service of the land; also they give glimpses of which Powers were invoked and what rites were performed as the seasons passed.[15]

Bede says that the Anglii of the ancient times divided the year into only two seasons: summer and winter. These were divided by moon-lives, months, six to each season; but the year was governed by the sun. The two greatest festivals were at the two Solstices, Midsummer and Midwinter. These times were so important that each was 'guarded' by two moons: *Ærra Liða*, the month before Midsummer and *Æftera Liða*, the month after Midsummer – **June** and **July**; *Ærra Geola* (Yule) and *Æftera Geola* flanking Midwinter – **December** and **January**. (see calendar page 45)

Winter began with the first full moon in **October**, which was called *Winterfylleþ* (*Wintirfylliþ* in Bede's spelling) for that reason. The writers on the *computus* in old English explain *Liða* as being formed from the verb *liðan*, to travel, especially by sea, since in the months of **June** and **July** the weather is calm and most pleasant and safe for voyages. Yet Bede's explanation that *Wintirfylliþ* – 'winter full moon' – is the equivalent of *hiems plenilunium*, shows that *Liða* must mean moon. If so, it must have been a sacred name, too holy – or too pagan – for common use and Christian explanation.

---

[15] The relevant information from the works of Bede and the early English scholars who followed him has been extracted and quoted under the names of the months, in an *An Anglo-Saxon Dictionary*, J. Bosworth and T. N. Toller, O.U.P.

Three months were simply characterised by what they brought to the farmer's notice.

February 'Fill-dyke' was *Sol-monaþ*, Mud Month.

May was *Þri-milce*, Three Milkings – "for ðon swylce genihtsumnes wæs geo on Brytone and eac on Germania lande, of ðæm Ongla ðeod com on þas Breotone, ðæt hi on ðæm monðe þriwa on dæge mylcedon heora neat" (because there was such abundance of old in Britain, and also in Germany, whence the English nation came to Britain, that in that month they milked their cattle three times a day.) Was this a far-off memory of the easy days before the deterioration of the climate at the end of the Northern Bronze Age (500–400 BCE), or just the perpetual belief that things were always better once upon a time?

August was *Weod-monaþ*, Weed Month – "for ðon þe hi on ðam monþe mæst geweaxaþ" (because they grow most in that month).

Bede says that *Sol-monaþ* was popularly known as 'the month of cakes' – *mensis placentarum* – "which in that month the English offered to their gods." Ploughing had begun. These '*placentae*' were probably similar to the one placed in the first furrow towards the end of the *Æcerbot* ritual. The Latin word *placenta* is still used as a medical term for the organ to which the foetus is joined, which nourishes it in the womb and which comes away as the after-birth, Though Bede uses the vague expression 'their gods', the divinity to whom these cakes were offered would surely be '*Folde fira modor*', Earth Mother of mankind, Terra Mater, Nerthus.

March is the month of Mars, the Roman god of war. To the early English, however, it was not *Tiwes-monaþ* but *Hreð-monaþ*, Hreð's Month – "*a dea illorum Rheda, cui in illo sacrificabant, nominatur*" (named from their goddess Rheda, to whom they sacrificed in that month). As a common noun, *hreð* in Old English means 'glory, fame, triumph, honour', particularly as gained from military exploits. As an adjective, *hreðe* means 'fierce, cruel, rough', words that can describe the March winds as well as warriors. Hreð was a wælcyrie; her month was the last month of winter.

Next came **April** – *Eostre-monaþ* , Eostre's Month, the first month of spring by English reckoning. In the Germanic languages the name is related to 'east', more precisely 'from the east'. It is cognate with the word 'dawn' in other Indo-European languages, for example in Sanskrit, Greek, Latin and Lithuanian. Eostre was the goddess of the dawn and also of the spring equinox, which comes at the end of her name-month. After the equinox, the sun annexes more and more of the kingdom of the night; this time is to the year what full sunrise is to the day.

The sequence Hreð – Eostre has the same significance in early English mythological symbolism as the right-hand side of Botticelli's great painting *Primavera*, where wild, wind-blown Chloris is being superseded by – or rather transformed into – the poised, flower-bedecked Flora.

September was *Halig-monaþ*, Holy Month – "for ðon ðe ure yldran, ða ða hi hæðene wæron, on ðam monþe hi guldon hiora deofolgeldum" (because our ancestors, when they were heathen, paid their devil-tribute in that month). Later, the name *Hærfest-monaþ*, Harvest Month was substituted, as having less obviously heathen implications. It was in September that the German visitors met the Harvest Queen on her wagon among her rejoicing subjects and recognised her as the goddess Ceres.

If the English had a separate name for Earth Mother in her harvest aspect, this might have been a name formed from the verbs *gifan*, to give, or *gifian*, to bestow gifts, such as Giefu, grace, favour; Gifole, generous, bountiful; Gifiende, bestowing gifts. Such a name would be related to the Norse Gefn, giver, a by-name of Freya and to Gefjon, the giving one. In the ancient times, when the gods first came to the northlands, Gefjon ploughed out a large chunk of southern Sweden and towed it away south across the ocean. She brought it to the east coast of the Cimbric peninsula and gave it to the votaries of Nerthus. It became the island of Sillende (Danish Sjaelland) which may have been the centre of the Nerthus cult. Gefjon settled down there *and married Scyld*!

November was *Blot-monaþ*, the Month of Sacrifice – "Forðon ure yldran, ða hy hæðene wæron, on þam monþe hi bleotan a, ðæt is, ðæt hy betæhton and benemdon hyra deofolgyldum ða neat ða ðe hy woldon syllan" (because our ancestors, when they were heathen, always sacrificed in this month; that is, they assigned and dedicated to their idols the cattle that they purposed to offer up). This happened at the great annual slaughtering of the cattle that could not be over-wintered. So the folk could honour their gods, then spend the dark days feasting on roast meat, keeping up their strength and their spirits.

The power unleashed at the Midsummer Solstice must have been too strong and dangerous for Bede and his successors even to mention the rituals. As there was no major feast of the church at that time there was no need to dwell on the date. The church put the day under the powerful protection of St John the Baptist, whose message was repentance of sins. As it was originally a fire festival, there was an association of ideas.

"Midsummer Eve is counted or called the Witches Night and still in many places on St John's Night they make fires on the hills; but the Civil Wars coming on have put all these rites and customs quite out of fashion."[16]

However, Bede did have something to say about the Midwinter festival. The most sacred night, when the new Year began, was called *Modranect*, Mothers' Night. 'Modra' is plural; it was the night 'of the Mothers' not 'of the Mother'. He says that it was so called from the ceremonies which took place then; he does not describe them, nor does he say who the Mothers were.

In the old Roman provinces of Germania Inferior and Germania Superior, which lay north and south along the Rhine, there are many altars and votive stones with Latin inscriptions to groups of protective goddesses called *matres* (mothers) or *matronae* (matrons). Often they are linked to a tribe: *Matribus Suebis*, to the Suebian Mothers; or have names including the element *gabia* (giving, cognate with Gefn and Gefjon): *Matronibus Alagabiabus*, to the All-giving Matrons.

The Anglii were living far out of reach of any society where folk commissioned Latin dedications to Germanic Mothers. We know the name of one Mother whom they honoured: *Terra Mater* Earth Mother. The *Æcerbot* also calls on the Mother of Earth:

"*Erce, erce, erce, eorþan modor*"

There are two theories about *Erce*: that it is the name of an otherwise unknown goddess who was Earth's mother; or that it is a ritual cry, otherwise unrecorded and of unknown meaning.

In fact, *erce* does exist in Old English. It is one of the spellings of the Greek prefix αρχι, as in *arch*angel, *arch*bishop, etc. The native equivalent was *heah*, high; *erce-biscop* and *heah-biscop* were both used, seemingly

---

[16] The antiquary John Aubrey (1626–97) gathered and made notes on a mass of material which remained unpublished at his death. One of his collections was on '*The Remains of Gentilism*' (Paganism) '*and Judaism*'; it was much plundered by later antiquaries and finally published by the Folklore Society in 1880. This quotation illustrates 'the remains of paganism' in seventeenth century England. However much we may disagree with the Puritan opposition to maypoles, mince pies etc., they were much closer to the old religion, and much more aware of its survival than most folk in the twentieth century.

according to the fancy of the write. Greek was known and taught in early England. During the last quarter of the seventh century, the Archbishop of Canterbury was a Greek, Theodore of Tarsus (d. 690). The Old English magico-medical texts often use foreign words and phrases, often in defiance of their original grammar and strangely garbled in form, their exotic look and sound giving them extra potency.

So *erce* might be used in this line in the sense of 'High One!' or 'Exalted One!'; the effect would be like the three-fold *sanctus* in "Sanctus, Sanctus, Sanctus, Dominus Deus Sabaoth".

What is exalted high above earth is heaven, so the Mother of the Earth Goddess would be Queen of Heaven, the Lady of all Ladies – and we do know who she is.

The tribes of the Suebic confederation were the southern neighbours of the English. Later native sources named the Eider as the frontier with the *Swaefe*, or Old Saxons. Referring to the Suebi, Tacitus reports the startling information that a section of them worshipped Isis. He seems to have been taken aback by this, because he goes on:

> "I have found out all too little about this foreign cult, except that the emblem itself, which is fashioned like a Liburnian galley, shows that the rite is imported."[17]

In fact, it shows nothing of the kind. The Liburnian was the light, fast-moving vessel of the Roman fleet; the northern rock-pictures show that a light slender boat had been a ritual object among the Baltic people for over a thousand years before Tacitus wrote.

Whatever ceremony these Suebi were performing in honour of their goddess, it reminded the Romans of the 'ship of Isis' ritual.[18] By the end of the first century, Isis was not just a goddess of the Egyptians. In the second century *Transformations of Lucius Apuleius*, known as *The Golden Ass*, the goddess Isis proclaims herself to be "Nature, the universal mother, mistress of all

---

[17] Germania ch. 9.

[18] *The Golden Ass*, Apuleius ch. 18. The text is given with the 1566 translation into lively Elizabethan English by W. Adlington. This version was probably read, enjoyed, and recalled by Shakespeare when he was writing *A Midsummer Night's Dream*. Apuleius has also been translated into clear modern English, with an interesting introduction, by Robert Graves, Penguin Classics 1950.

elements, primordial child of time."[19] Then she recites all the goddess-names by which she is invoked throughout the Mediterranean lands and the Near East: she is Artemis (Diana), the virgin-huntress; Aphrodite (Venus), the desiring and desired; Hecate, the witch; Proserpina, the spring-bride; Juno, the queen, and so on.

The Germans called her Frija. This is a very ancient name from an Indo-European root, cognate with *priya*, beloved one, in Sanskrit. It is also cognate with the Old English *frig* or *frigu*, sexual intercourse. In English, the idea that there was something essentially vicious about sex, or that it entailed the debasement of women, was not native and was very slow to develop. There is a delightful seventeenth century quotation in the *Oxford English Dictionary* under the heading 'prick':

> "One word alone hath troubled some, because the immodest maid, soothing the young man, calls him her Prick... He who cannot away with this, instead of 'my Prick', let him write 'my Sweetheart'." (1671)[20]

The tone of this comment implies that in 1671, folk who objected to using the word prick in translations, as an endearment, were being needlessly squeamish. Possibly, the fact that the word for sex had also been the name of a goddess had a longer psychological influence than we realise.

However, in Old English, as well as in Old Saxon, the name of the goddess was also cognate with the word for a high-born lady: *freo*. This, in turn, is linked with the words *freond*, friend and *freondscip*, friendship. These were not the rather cool terms that they have become in Modern English. They were used in contexts where we would say 'passion', 'romantic love' or 'devotion'.

So the name of the goddess contained a range of different feelings and behaviour in a spectrum from rank lust, through yearning, tenderness, fidelity to queenly dignity.

Later Scandinavian mythology polarised the two extremes and made two great goddesses. Frigg, the wife of Odin, is the queen and devoted, sorrowing mother; Freya is the object of desire, the whore, the sorceress. It

---

[19] *The Golden Ass* ch. 17; Robert Graves's translation.

[20] *The Oxford English Dictionary* entry under 'prick': substantive IV, 17.

is either ironic, or very subtle, that the queen should be called Frigg (the beloved, desired) and the witch-whore should be called Freya (the lady).

When the German gods were aligned with Roman deities, Frija was identified with the Roman Venus: our Friday, *Frige-daeg*, is the Latin *Dies Veneris*, Venus's day.

The English were well aware of the two aspects of the great goddess, but they did not split her in two. In the late tenth century, the Christian homilist Ælfric referred to her as 'the shameless goddess', identifying her with Venus and making it clear that he thought of her as deified lust. Yet in the thirteenth century poem *Brut*, the first surviving great work to be composed in English after the Norman invasion, the poet Layamon has Hengest say this:

> *"We have a lady who is most high and mighty,*
> *High she is and holy; nobles love her for this:*
> *She is called Frea, well does she direct them...*
> *Frea, our Lady; we give to her Friday...*
> *So spoke Hengest, of all knights the handsomest..."*[21]

In this passage, the Lady is very much the high queen, though the reference to Friday as her holy day shows that the link with Venus is not forgotten.

It may be argued that both these references are very late, Ælfric was writing at a time when there was a second incursion of heathen Vikings. Layamon's poem, though its most powerful and imaginative passages were added by himself, was an extensive re-working of a Norman-French translation of Geoffrey of Monmouth's *Historia Regum Britanniae*.

However, the Lady's name had already become part of the English landscape, and this must have happened long before. Friden in Derbyshire was *Frigeden*, her valley; Fretherne in Gloucestershire was *Friðorne*, her thorn-tree; the Freefolk of Hampshire were *Frigefolc*, her people; Froyle in the same county was *Freohyll*, her hill.[22]

---

[21] *Brut* 11.6943–6952 translated with notes and introduction, R. Allen, Dent 1992.

[22] *The Oxford Dictionary of English Placenames* E. Ekwall 1960.
This can be followed up in greater detail in the county collections published by the English Place-Name Society.
cont. next page

It is interesting to note that *freo* survived in English as late as the end of the fourteenth century, as a word for a high-born, gracious lady. In *Sir Gawain and the Green Knight*, the poet refers to the lovely, dangerous temptress as '*þæt fre*' and Gawain himself calls her '*my fre*', when she has come to his bed and is attacking him with all the powers of Freo in both her aspects.[23]

It is often pointed out that a place-name containing the name of one of the old gods is not by itself a proof that there was once a temple, a shrine or a ritual in that place.

Physical proof that there were once temples or shrines in any place in England is almost non-existent. There is a site of one small hall at Yeavering, that was probably allowed to survive as a Christian chapel, in accordance with Pope Gregory's advice to the missionaries. King Raedwald put up a Christian altar in his family shrine, presumably at or near Rendlesham, which remained long enough for King Aldwulf (663-713) to have seen it when he was a boy. King Edwin's temple at Goodmanham was desecrated and burned at the orders of its own high priest.[24]

Yet the shrines and holy places of the old tradition can be seen everywhere in England. Tacitus says of the early Germans:

"They judge that gods cannot be contained inside walls nor can the greatness of the heavenly ones be represented in the likeness of any human face: they consecrate groves and woodland glades and call

---

Ekwall was not quite sure that Friden had been named for the goddess but the form *Frigeden*, dating from the reign of King Edgar, has since been found. (See *Women in Anglo-Saxon England* p. 28, C. Fell 1984.)

[23] *Sir Gawain and the Green Knight* ed. J. R. R. Tolkien and E. V. Gordon 1972: 11.1545 and 1549, also Glossary '*fre*'.

[24] (a) The 'church' at Yeavering: *Yeavering*, B. Hope-Taylor; D.O.E. Archaeological Report no. 7, H.M.S.O. 1977. See references to Building D2, the 'temple/church', especially pp. 277–9 on the conversion to Christian use.

(b) Rædwald's temple: *Historia Ecclesiastica Gentis Anglorum*, Bk. II ch. 15, Bede. Text and translation in Loeb Classical Library no. 146; translation and notes by L. Sherley-Price: *A History of the English Church and People*, Penguin Classics 1968.

(c) Edwin's temple: H.E.G.A. Bk. II ch. 13.

by the names of 'gods' that mystery which they only perceive by their sense of reverence"[25]

– as the priest of Nerthus sensed her presence in the shrine. The holiest place in Old Anglia was a secluded lake in a consecrated grove and such places in England are just as numinous:

> *"At a sprynge wel under a thorn*
> *Ther was bote of bale, a lytel here aforn:*
> *Ther beside stant a mayde*
> *Fulle of love y-bounde.*
> *Ho-so wol seche truwe love*
> *Yn hyr hyt schal be founde."*

At the source of a spring under a hawthorn tree there was a cure for sorrow (or, a remedy for evil) a little while ago. Beside them (the well and the tree) stands a young girl (or, a virgin) full of love, held fast by love. Whoever wants to seek for true love (or, real love) will find it in her.

This little lyric was written down at the end of the fourteenth century and has been fitted into a Christian context: confession will give a penitent access to the Well of Salvation, which was opened up for mankind by the wound in the side of Christ Crucified. The hawthorn tree suggests the crown of thorns, and the maiden could be Mary keeping her vigil by the cross. Yet though the poem will carry these symbols intellectually, it sounds, and feels, much more like a visit to one of Freo's holy places – Fretherne in Gloucestershire? – or a night-watch in the spring woods to welcome Eostre when she comes at sunrise, than it does a vigil on Calvary.

One editor, R. T. Davies says: "The healing and holy well, the thorn and the maiden who stands beside, have a mysterious resonance that suggests their connection with popular lore rather than with the tradition of the learned." Though it is three hundred years later than the Norman invasion that brought a huge influx of French and Latin into the English vocabulary, every word of it is from Old English.[26]

---

[25] Germania ch.9.

[26] *Medieval English Lyrics* ed. R. T. Davies, Faber & Faber 1963; text on p. 212, editor's note p. 350.

When names like *Frigeden* and *Friðorne* were given, people did not name places after gods in which they did not believe, like an eighteenth century landowner calling his neo-classical summer-house 'Apollo's Temple'. And no English Christian, from 597 to 1066, would ever give such names.

Therefore we could assume just from place-names, that the three great gods mentioned by Tacitus as being worshipped in first century Germany were being worshipped by the English in their new home and that they felt these powers emanating from the land. The three gods are set in our landscape and printed on our maps: Wednesbury, Woden's stronghold, near Wolverhampton; the great Wansdyke, Woden's earthwork, near the Vale of Pewsey; Thundersley, Thunor's sacred grove, in Essex; Tuesley, Tiw's sacred grove, in Surrey.

The surviving material proof that the early English trusted these gods can be found in our museums. That is, the fact that they put themselves under these gods' protection in life and in death. They put the Tiw rune ᛏ on their swords; they wore Thunor's hammer as an amulet and took it with them to their graves; Thunor's fylfot cross was stamped on their cremation urns. High-born warriors wore the sign of the Woden devotee, the spear-dancer, on their helmet- plates and brooches.

However, to judge by their religious emblems, there was another very famous god – famous, that is, in Norse mythology – whose protection had been sought and valued by the English long before the Vikings came to England. They protected themselves with the boar-emblem. The boar stands on the crest of the Benty Grange helmet; boars are worked in gold and garnets on the shoulder-clasps of the Sutton Hoo armour. When Beowulf and his companions landed in Denmark, they were wearing boar-emblems on their helmets:

> *"Eoforlic scionon
> ofer hleorbergan gehroden golde,
> fah ond fyrheard, ferhwearde heold."*

Boar-shapes shone above the cheek-guards, adorned with gild, bright and fire-hardened, kept guard over life.[27]

After his victory, Beowulf was given many treasures by the Danish king, including a golden standard with a boar emblem: *'eofor heafodsegn'*.

---

[27] *Beowulf* 11. 303–5.

In Norse myth and ritual, the boar was the symbol of Frey (the Lord). He is described as "the most glorious of the Æsir. He is *ruler of rain and sunshine and thus of the produce of the earth*." Rain and sunshine come from the heavens; these details indicate which god the English priests and healers had first invoked as the heavenly bridegroom of Earth Mother and the begetter of her children:

> *"Hal wes þu, folde, fira modor*
> *Beo þu growende on godes fæðme,*
> *fodre gefylled firum to nytte."*

Hail to thee, earth, Mother of mortals, may you grow big in God's embrace, filled with food for the use of humankind.

Frey was a fertility god: his image at Uppsala had a huge penis, like the stick-men of the rock-pictures.

The boar and the sow were also emblems of Frey's lovely and amorous sister Freya who, according to Snorri, had *Syr* (Sow) as one of her names. She had so many names because, like Isis, she travelled far and wide among foreign peoples. A thousand years before Snorri, Tacitus described the Baltic Æstii, whose rites and behaviour were Suebic, though their language was not:

> "They worship the Mother of the Gods. As an emblem of the rite, they bear the shapes of wild boars. This (boar) avails more than weapons or human protection; it guarantees that the worshipper of the goddess is without fear even when surrounded by enemies."[28]

At Yule-tide, Norse warriors made their vows for the coming year on Frey's sacrificial boar; it seems that he was the Lord of the winter feasts. In England, we still make resolutions for the New Year; for centuries before the turkey arrived, the boar's head had the place of honour at Yule-tide feasts and we still sing a carol that accompanied its processional entry into the feasting-hall. Every year there are complaints about excessive eating and drinking at Christmas; though the state religion does not provide fertility orgies, the office party keeps the tradition alive.

Yet there seems to be no evidence that a god *Frea* was ever worshipped by that name in England. That is partly because the English knew it was not a personal name; the word is only used as meaning 'lord', so they could use it of Christ, they could use it of human kings and chiefs.

---

[28] *Germania* ch. 45.

Moreover, they knew what this particular Lord's name was. He was called Ing, the same form as the Old English patronymic. In the oldest Germanic legend of origins, Ing is one of the three sons of Mannus, the primal human off-spring, born from the androgynous Tuisto who came from the Earth. So Ing was a *Son of Man*; the Ingaevones, the tribes of the north German coastlands, including the English, were his descendants.[29]

In Sweden, Ingvi-Frey was worshipped with the same kind of ceremonies as the Anglian Nerthus, only with the sexes reversed. His image went round in a waggon during the autumn and winter; wherever it stopped there was feasting and revelling; it was attended by a priestess, who was looked on as the god's wife.

It is significant that Ing ᛝ is the only god-name from the original Germanic fuþark that has been allowed to remain unaltered in the tenth century English *Rune Poem*.[30] *(for runes see page 50)*

The alterations to the other two god-names have been made with care and respect; in the Elizabethan sense, they are witty. The original meaning of the runes is clearly signalled; even the original god-names have been smuggled in by means of bi-lingual puns.

The seventeenth rune is *Tir* ᛏ. Originally it was Tiw, from **teiwaz* in primitive Germanic. The *Rune Poem* says:

> *"Tir biþ tacna sum, healdeð trywa wel*
> *wiþ æþelingas, a biþ on færylde*
> *ofer nihta genipu næfre swiceþ."*

Tir is one of the signs (*tacn* can mean a sign of the Zodiac; a sign of the future, a prognostic; a supernatural sign; an emblem or standard) keeps faith well with princes, is always on course above the night-fogs; it never fails in its duty.

---

[29] Germania ch. 2.

[30] The text of the *Rune Poem* is in A.S.P.R. vol. VI. The text with a translation and discussion can be found in *Poems of Wisdom and Learning in Old English* T. A. Shippey, Brewer 1976; also in *Anglo-Saxon Verse Runes* L. Rodrigues, Llanerch 1992.

Detailed studies of the runes and their uses can be found in:
Runes: an Introduction R. W. V. Elliott, Manchester U.P. 1959.
An Introduction to English Runes R. I. Page, Methuen 1973.

Tiw was identified with Mars, who is both a god of war and a planet. Planets and signs of the Zodiac are used for prognostication. The sign of Mars ♂ includes a ⟙ –shaped element. *Tir* as a common noun in Old English means 'glory, honour', qualities which were most appropriate to princes and won in war. *Tyr* is the Norse equivalent of Tiw; he was the god who sacrificed his sword-hand by putting it as a pledge into the mouth of the wolf Fenrir while the other gods were chaining him. As soon as the wolf knew he had been trapped, he bit off the hand; Tyr had known from the first that this must happen. Tir is like enough in sound to Tyr, so by using it, the essential meaning of the rune can be kept and the god discreetly named.

The fourth rune ᚩ is *Os* (O). The *Rune Poem* stanza is a clever little exercise in bi-lingual double meaning:

> *"Os byþ ordfruma ælcre spræce,*
> *wisdomes wraþu and witena frofur*
> *and eorla gehwam eadnys and tohiht."*

In Old English *os* means god. In Latin *os* means mouth.

> *The god is the origin of all eloquence,*
> *mainstay of wisdom and comfort of the wise,*
> *the prosperity of every hero.*

> *The mouth is the source of all speech,*
> *mainstay of wisdom and comfort of the wise,*
> *the prosperity of every man.*

Os was cognate with *As* in Norse, where it meant one of the Æsir, the chief family of gods. In Old English, it could be used as an element in first names: Osric, Oswald, Osmund, etc. but it was not used as a word to refer to the God of the Christians. Woden was equated with Mercury, the god of eloquence (among other things). The tales about the Norse Odin tell how he gave one of his eyes as the price of wisdom; he also won the mead of poetic inspiration. Luckily for Christian rune-masters, the Latin word 'os' could be substituted without ruining the sense, to keep the outward form of the rune-name without obviously referring to Woden.

However, there is no substitution for the name of Ing, the twenty-second rune ᛜ (Ng) and the ritual emblem is referred to without disguise:

"Ing wæs ærest mid Est-Denum
gesewen secgum, oþ he siððan est
ofer wæg gewat; wæn æfter ran;
þus heardingas þone hæle nemdun."

Ing was first seen among men among the East-Danes, till he later departed east over the sea; the wain ran after; thus the warriors named the hero.

The Danes had moved south from Skåne into Sillende and the other eastern islands during the late fourth and early fifth centuries. These Danes were now east of Angeln. Sillende was Gefjon's island; H. M. Chadwick suggested that here was the location of the Nerthus ritual. A place-name recorded in the twelfth century, Niartharum, contains the Danish form of her name. The wain suggests her ritual waggon; its following the god 'over the wave' recalls how the waggon went back to the island and the sacred grove. The statement that it 'ran after' the god seems less strange in the light of the information from *Germania* that Nerthus was only present in her waggon when she chose and for as long as she chose. Her priest had to be able to sense her presence and her absence. Departing eastwards across the Baltic would bring the god to the land of the Æstii, where the Mother of the Gods was worshipped as supreme.

It is easy to understand why Bede did not go into details about what happened on Modranect. If the English were already celebrating a young Lord (Frea), Ing son of Mannus, and his Divine Mother at the same time as the feast of the Nativity, the parallels would seem too close, blasphemous even, to a theologian like Bede, though they have not seemed so to most English people, then or now.

Perhaps the word 'conversion' is inappropriate when it is used about the particular religion of Old Anglia and England. The English did not 'turn' from the Son and the Mother. They seem to have been interested to hear fresh news about them when the messengers arrived from the south in 597. My belief is that for the early English, the good news, *god-spell*: gospel, was that everyone – regardless of rank, sex or dying passively in bed of sickness or old age – was invited to the banquet in the royal feasting-hall of heaven. It was wonderful to learn that this great favour had been won for them by their young hero, their *Frea*:

"Geseah ic þa Frean mancynnes
efstan elne micle þæt He me wolde on gestigan ...
Ongyrede Hine þa geong hæleð þæt wæs God ælmihtig,
strang and stiðmod; gestah He on gealgan heanne..."

Then I saw [the Cross is speaking] the Lord of mankind hasten with great courage so that he might mount upon me . . . the young hero stripped himself, strong and resolute; he ascended the high gallows...[31]

Of the other three great gods, Tiw, Woden and Thunor, the one who remained as the most powerful abiding presence after the coming of Christianity, was Woden. He remained as the royal ancestor in the genealogies; as the lord of magic, the shaman; and as the leader of the Wild Hunt.

One of the most powerful episodes in Norse poetry is Odin's description of how he hung on the World Tree for nine nights, buffeted by high winds, starving and pierced by a spear, "myself sacrificed to myself" until, staring into the abyss, he seized the runes and fell screaming.[32]

However, in the stanzas that follow, he does not recite the twenty-four runes of the original *fuþark*, but eighteen (2x9) spells for chanting, speaking or whispering. Two of them: the second, for the use of healers and the twelfth, for bringing hanged corpses down from the gallows and giving them the power of speech, include the use of runes. The sixth is a counter-charm, for turning the power of hostile runes back against the enemy who cut them. The power of the tenth charm, against hags, was being used by English healers centuries before it was listed in the Icelandic manuscript of Eddic lays.

The fourth charm is for the use of prisoners of war: if it is chanted, his chains will break and fall from his limbs. The Eddic poem does not mention runes; but we learn from a story told by Bede that this technique of escaping was known in seventh century England and that here it did involve the use of runes:

---

[31] *The Dream of the Rood* ll. 33–4, ed. with introduction and notes M. Swanton, Exeter U.P. 1987; text and parallel verse translation by R. Hamer in *A Choice of Anglo-Saxon Verse* pp.159–171, Faber & Faber 1970.

[32] *Havamal* sts 138–164. There is a translation with useful notes in *The Poetic Edda* pp. 36–40, L. M. Hollander, Texas U.P. 1962.

The Battle of the Trent, between the Northumbrians and the Mercians was fought in 679. Though the Northumbrians had not suffered a crushing disaster, they had been forced to withdraw. A young Northumbrian nobleman called Imma had been struck down and lay stunned among a heap of corpses. When he came to himself, the battle was over; he dragged himself to his feet and set off to find the Northumbrian troops. Unluckily, the first men he met were Mercians, who took him to their chief. Imma guessed, rightly, that if he admitted he was a fighting-man of high rank, he would be killed; the Mercian chief had kindred blood to avenge. So he said he was a poor churl who had been pressed into service to bring up supplies. The Mercians gave him some treatment for his wounds, while they waited to see if he was worth keeping or selling as a slave. He began to get stronger, so he was chained up at night in case he tried to escape but, as soon as his guards left him, the fetters fell off. The Mercian chief immediately asked Imma if he had got any '*litteras solutorias*' that he was keeping hidden.[33]

Bede was writing for Latin scholars and kept his style pure of barbarisms. He used words meaning 'loosening, freeing, untying letters'; the phrase is given in Leo Sherley-Price's translation as 'written charms'. When Bede's *Historia Ecclesiastica Gentis Anglorum* was turned into Old English, the Mercian chief's question was put into words that show exactly what he and his men had in mind: "*hwæðer he þa alysendlecan rune cuðe and þa stafas mid him awritene hæfde*" whether he knew loosening runes and had the carved staves with him.

Bede had no intention of advertising the power and practical efficiency of runes. He called the stories that were told about them '*fabulae*' fables. In his tale, the captive had a brother who was a Christian priest. Believing Imma to be dead, he was saying masses to free his soul from torment. As he was not dead, his body was being set free as the next best favour.

However, the Mercians' first thought, when hearing about fetters that seemingly unchained themselves, was not 'masses' but 'loosening runes'.

Woden appears as the divine healer and master of rune magic in the *Nigon Wyrta Galdor*, the Nine Herbs Charm, which refers openly to the

---

[33] Bede: *H.E.G.A.* Bk IV ch. 23.

god's self-sacrifice by hanging.[34] This charm is also interesting because it entails the use of a technique practised by the Lappish and other Finno-Ugric peoples of the north: the healer fights a spirit-combat against the spirit of the disease at the same time as she or he is preparing and administering the bodily treatment.

A wound has become infected, it is probably inflamed or suppurating. The healer prepares a salve of nine herbs (actually, eight herbs as we use the term and a crab apple which sacrifices itself heroically to destroy the poison on coming in contact with it). These herbs have to be pounded and mixed to a paste with water, ashes, beaten egg and the juice of the apple. As each herb is added, it is heartened and cheered on to the fight, as Hildgyð encourages Waldere, by being reminded of its powers and past exploits. Six herbs have already been added when the healer sees the spirit of the infection in the form of a serpent coming towards the sickbed:

> *"Wyrm com snican, toslat he man.*
> *Þa genam Woden VIIII wuldortanas,*
> *sloh ða þa næddran þæt heo on VIIII tofleah."*

A serpent came crawling, it tore someone's flesh. Then Woden took nine glory-twigs; he struck the snake, so that it flew apart into nine pieces.

The healer re-enacts Woden's seizing of the runes by having nine wooden sticks with the initial rune of each herb's name cut into them. By doing this, the healer takes on the power of Woden, just as the staves have taken into themselves the power of the runes and the powers of the herbs. So it is Woden who strikes the poison-spirit and shatters it into fragments.

When the two most powerful herbs, chervil and fennel, are added to the salve, an amazing claim is made for them:

> *"Fille ond finule, felamihtigu twa:*
> *þa wyrte gesceop witig drihten,*
> *halig on heofonum, þa he hongode;*
> *sette and sænde on VII worulde*
> *earum and eadigum eallum to bote..."*

---

[34] See references in footnote 2 above.

Chervil and fennel, very powerful pair: the wise Lord, holy in heaven, created these herbs while he was hanging; he set them and sent them into the seven worlds as a help to all, poor and rich.

By mentally adding "on the cross" after *he hongode*, a discreet pretence could be made that this was an act of special creation by Christ at the Crucifixion but everyone who knew the Gospels would be aware that this was not so. Though the charm later states that "Crist stod ofer adle ængancundes", Christ stood over disease of every kind – which the Gospels would endorse – it is clear that the gift to mankind of chervil and fennel, like the gift of the runes, is seen as coming from Woden's passion, not Christ's.

The Wild Hunt was originally made up of the souls of dead warriors riding to Valhalla to join Woden's host of champions, waiting for the last battle against the forces of destruction. In modern German, the Wild Hunt is also known as the Wild Army; in the Middle Ages, Germans called it *Wuotanes her*, Woden's army. In later English folklore, it is usually taken to be the souls of the restless dead, often with some notorious local sinner leading them, being hunted by the hounds of hell. Rationalist explanations include the terrifying violence of the spring and autumn gales, also the cries of flocks of migrating geese.

The most vivid description of the Wild Hunt in Old English comes from Peterborough Abbey in 1127. This abbey was the last centre in England where the *Anglo-Saxon Chronicle* was still being written.

In 1127, the monks had just had an unpleasant French abbot imposed on them. They had been enduring foreign abbots since 1070, when William appointed the violent Turold. His outstanding quality in that king's eyes was that he made a better soldier than a monk. He needed to be; Hereward was leading the English resistance in those parts.

The new abbot of Peterborough was called Henry of Poitou; the chronicler says bitterly;

"Everything he could take, he sent overseas. He did nothing for the monastery's welfare and left nothing untouched. Let no one be surprised at the truth of what we are about to relate, for it was general knowledge throughout the whole country that immediately after his arrival – it was Sunday, 6th February – many men both saw and heard a great number of huntsmen hunting. The huntsmen were black, huge and hideous, and rode on black horses and he-goats, and their hounds were jet-black, with eyes like saucers and horrible. This was seen in the very deer-park of the town of Peterborough and in all the woods that stretch from that same town to Stamford [this was the great forest of the *Bruneswald*; Bromswold in modern place-names] and in the night the monks heard them sounding and winding their horns. Reliable witnesses, who kept watch in the night, declared that there might be as many as twenty or thirty of them winding their horns, as near as they might tell. This was seen from the time of his (Abbot Henry's) arrival, all through Lent and right up to Easter. Such was his entrance; of his exit we cannot yet say."[35]

It is very clear what exit the English monk was hoping for: the huge riders, the he-goat mounts, the jet-black, saucer-eyed hounds are meant to sound diabolical, with the implication that the devil has come for his own. Yet, what do these hellish huntsmen actually do in the woods? No babies are eaten alive, no victims torn limb from limb, no fire and brimstone. They hunt – they have a good time in the forest, as free-born Englishmen had always done until the Normans imposed their hellish forest laws.

Within living memory of 1127, the most famous hunter in the Bruneswald had been Hereward himself. He made it his base when Ely was betrayed to the Normans after the famous year-long siege; from its depths he pounced on Norman barons, tormented Norman bishops and abbots, just like his spiritual successor, Robin Hood.

A band of dissidents – outlaws or freedom-fighters or even disgruntled monks – might well have found it amusing to stage a Wild Hunt, to mock or terrorise an unpopular magnate. Blackened faces or masks would protect their identity as well as add to the terror. But blackened faces and strange happenings at night go back a long way in Germanic tradition.

Tacitus writes of a tribe called the Harii; the word means 'army' in Germanic. He places them somewhere between the upper Oder and the upper Vistula, so they would be Gothic or Vandalic and far out of personal contact with the Romans. The details which reached Tacitus about their way of fighting sound distinctly odd:

---

[35] *The Anglo-Saxon Chronicle* (Dent no. 1624) pp. 257–8.

"The Harii, apart from the strength in which they surpass the tribes thus listed, are fierce in nature and trick out their innate ferocity by the help of art and choice of time: they *blacken* their shields and *dye* their bodies; they choose *pitchy nights* for their battles and strike fear into their enemies by the terrifying and shadowy appearance of *an army of the dead*. No enemy is able to withstand this unaccustomed and seemingly *hellish apparition*; in every battle they are defeated at first sight."[36]

Indeed it must have been horrific the first time it happened; but surely the novelty would wear off after a while. Also, if it was so effective a method of winning battles, why did the other tribes not adopt similar tactics?

So it has been suggested that the Harii, who appeared like "an army of the dead" were not a tribe but a cult association of warriors dedicated to Woden, like the later berserks. These nightly activities would be their rituals, possibly worked up to frenzied ecstasy and designed to frighten strangers away. If this is so, then there was a beautiful aptness about the reports that came from the Bruneswald that Lent in 1127.

To the early English, the world was full of lesser spirits as well as the great gods. The charm *Wiþ Færstice* against a sudden stitch or rheumatic pain gives a vivid glimpse of some of these other beings. Sudden stabs of pain with no visible source, such as a wound or a broken bone, were thought to come from invisible weapons hurled by supernatural enemies. In this charm, the healer is making a herbal poultice boiled in butter and anointing the knife with which it will be applied and which will cut out the invisible spear-head lodged in the victim's body. At the same time. he gets ready for a spirit-combat with the attackers, whom he can hear and see:

"Hlude wæron hy, la hlude, ða hy ofer þone hlæw ridon
wæron anmode ða hy ofer land ridon ...
Stod under linde, under leohtum scylde
þær ða mihtigan wif hyra mægen beræddon
and hy gyllende garas sændon."

---

[36] Germania ch. 43

Loud were they, lo, loud when they rode over the burial-mound; they were fierce when they rode over the land ...I stood under the linden-wood, under a light shield where the mighty women put forth their powers and sent their yelling spears.[37]

This sounds like an attack by *wælcyrian*, valkyries; the lines would go well, recited to Wagner's music. However, just to make sure that the patient is protected from every possible assailant, the healer names, and so neutralises, other likely enemies: hags, hostile gods (the old word *os*, '*esa*' is used) and elves.

In early England, the frontier between this world and the other worlds – there were six others according to the Nine Herbs Charm – was not hard and fast; it was not always easy to know which side you were on or who was coming to meet you. During the second Danish war, when things were going very badly for England, Archbishop Wulfstan addressed a passionate sermon to the English people, denouncing them for their evil-doings, which he said were the cause of their defeats. He gave a list of contemporary English evil-doers: kinslayers, perjurers, murderers, whores, adulterers, plunderers, robbers, witches and *wælcyrian*. The other eight types were and are flesh and blood – so who were these tenth century English valkyries and what were they doing? Necromancy has been suggested: but there was a technical term for women who sought knowledge from the dead: *helrune*. Whatever they were doing, and whichever world they belonged to, Wulfstan expected his hearers to believe that *wælcyrian* were as effective in this world as any of the other malefactors he accused. It would sound odd to hear a modern churchman or social reformer demanding that our streets should be cleared of muggers, gun-men, drug pedlars, child-abusers and extra-terrestrials. The frontiers of the material world have been closed and more rigorously guarded since Wulfstan's time.

The early English were prepared to meet elves anywhere: there were elves in the hills, *dun-elfen*; in the springs, pools and water-courses, *wæter-elfen*; in the groves and forests, *wudu-elfen*; in the sea, *sæ-elfen*; out on the moors, *wylde-elfen*. The list is very similar to the one Shakespeare gives in *The Tempest*:

---

[37] See references in note 2 above.

41

"Ye elves of hills, brooks, standing lakes and groves;
And ye that on the sands with printless foot
Do chase the ebbing Neptune and do fly him
When he comes back..."

In the *Færstic* charm, elves are spiteful, just as willing and able to do harm as *wælcyrian*, hags and angry gods. As late as the nineteenth century, Neolithic arrow-heads were still known as 'elf-bolts'. In *Wuthering Heights*, Cathy Earnshaw senses, rightly, that her housekeeper, Nelly, is unsympathetic, even hostile to her. In her delirium she says:

"I see in you, Nelly, an aged woman; you have grey hair and bent shoulders. This bed is the fairy cave under Peniston Crag and you are gathering elf-bolts to hurt our heifers, pretending while I am near, that they are only locks of wool."

A little later, when she learns that Nelly has been telling tales about Heathcliff, she screams,

"You witch! So you do seek elf-bolts to hurt us!"[38]

In *Beowulf*, elves are spine-chilling creatures of darkness:

"Þanon untydras ealle onwocon,
eotenas ond ylfe ond orcneas..."[39]

Thence (from Caine's crime and exile) all evil births arose, etins and elves and monsters.

According to this poem, they are distant kin of Grendel. Yet the early English also saw elves as lovely. One of their words for women's surpassing beauty was *ælfscine*, elfin-bright, lovely as an elf.[40] Lovely elf-women, however, could be just as dangerous as the dark beings who lurked in the fens near Grendel's mere.

Some time about 1070, Eadric the Wild came upon some wood-elves not far from Bishop's Castle, in Shropshire. Eadric had been leading

---

[38] Wuthering Heights ch. 12.

[39] *Beowulf* ll. 111–2.

[40] For example, the elegant and steely heroine of *Judith* ed. B. J. Trimmer Exeter U.P. 1978.

the English resistance in the West Midlands but when the Danish fleet withdrew, the Northumbrians were crushed and Chester and Stafford fell, he made an honourable peace with William. By 1087, though, when the Domesday survey was complete, Eadric had vanished from the political scene and all his lands were in the hands of Normans, most of them in the hands of Roger Mortimer.

He had not vanished from the memory of the countryside. This is the tale that was told about him in Shropshire and Herefordshire, as it was written down near the end of the twelfth century by Walter Map, a scholar and courtier of Henry II:

Eadric was called 'Wild' which meant 'man of the woods' [Silvestris in Latin]. When folk left the homesteads and farmland for the forest, they were going beyond the protection of human laws and customs. He gained his by-name "from his nimbleness of body and his merry words and deeds" [He seems to be another spiritual forebear of Robin Hood, like Hereward.] He was a man of outstanding strength, courage and daring in battle.

He was in the woods at midnight, with only one lad for company, after a day's hunting during which he had got separated from the rest of his companions and had lost his way in the wilderness. He was drawing near to the edge of the forest when suddenly he heard music and saw the glimmer of lights. He made for the light, expecting to find a 'Guild-house' where he could shelter for the rest of the night. He came to a large building, but when he looked in, he saw that there were only women inside, "taller and more noble-looking than human women". They were dancing, wearing nothing but filmy shifts of the finest lawn.

One of these dancers was so outstandingly lovely that he became crazy with desire for her "though he had heard heathen fables about the troops of night-demons and companies of wood-nymphs" [Walter was writing in Latin; Old English would have said nihtgenga and wudu-elfen: goblins and wood-elves] "who took sudden vengeance on those who took them unawares."

Eadric was beyond caring about these dangers; he burst in and caught her up in his arms. All the other women set about him and there was a violent struggle but he won free, though both he and his page had suffered nasty damage to their legs and feet from the women's teeth and

43

nails. This sounds as if they were flesh and blood, like Wulfstan's wælcyrian – or that for some reason, Eadric was protected from or immune to their magic. None of them had an iron weapon.

He carried his prize away and took her home. During three days and nights of passionate love-making she kept unbroken silence, though she let him do everything he wanted. Then, on the fourth day, she spoke:

"Hail, my sweetest one – and hale shall you be, healthy and prosperous in everything you do, so long as you never taunt me about my sisters that you have snatched me from, or the place, the sacred grove I came from, or anything about it. But if you do, on that very day you will lose all your happiness. When I am gone, you will mourn your loss without end, till you bring your death on you because you cannot bear your grief."

So, of course, he bound himself by every oath he could think of that he would love her for ever and never do anything to displease her. He married her with great splendour; everyone who saw her said that her supreme loveliness was proof that she came from the elves. Yet they had a son.

And then, inevitably, he failed to keep his word. One night, he again came back late from hunting and she did not come to meet him. When he sent to look for her, she was nowhere to be found. He was tired, irritable, perhaps worried for her since they were living in wild and warlike times. So when she did at last appear, he scowled at her, then said sneeringly, "I suppose it was your sisters who kept you so long – " but before he could finish the cutting rebuke he had got ready for her, he found he was talking to the empty air, because at the word 'sisters' she vanished.

He was horrified when he realised what he had done; stabbed by agonising regret, he rushed back to the place where he had first seen her, but there was never another trace of her or her sisters. Day and night he called for her but all in vain. The agony could not go on for very long; self-neglect and sorrow soon wore his life away.

Yet, as late as the nineteenth century, there were folk in Shropshire who did not believe that Eadric was just bones in some nameless grave. They said that whenever a really serious war is coming to England, he rides out with his men as they used to ride out against the Normans, with his elf-woman returned to him, riding by his side. They always ride in the direction of the enemy country: they were seen going south when Napoleon was threatening invasion but they went northwards before the Crimean war with Russia.[41]

This is a good story, whether it comes from the Old English tradition or recent English invention. The original tale looks to the past and to the future – back to Woden's host of dead warriors; to Weland, who seized his swan-maiden, then lost her and never knew happiness again; to Siegfried, who was tricked into betraying his vows to his wise valkyrie and went to his destruction; but also forward to the enchantments of the medieval ballads and romances; to *A Midsummer Night's Dream*, *The Tempest and Comus*; to *La Belle Dame Sans Merci*; to *The Silmarillion* and *The Lord of the Rings*. And so on, as long as these beliefs and traditions can still stir our minds and our imaginations.

---

[41] There is a contemporary reference to Eadric, under the year 1067, in the Worcester Chronicle (*The Anglo-Saxon Chronicle* p. 200, G. N. Garmonsway). A few further details can be gleaned from the early post-Norman works, for example the *Historia Eccliastica* of the pro-English Ordericus Vitalis (1075–1143) who was born in Shropshire of an English mother and whose first tutor was an English priest called Siward; also the *Chronicon ex Chronicis* of Florence of Worcester (d. 1118). The story of the elf-woman comes from *De Nugis Curialium* (c. 1181) – Trifles, or Light Entertainment, for the Courtiers. The author, Walter Map (1140?–1209?) was a scholar, famous in his lifetime for his wit, a clerk of the royal household of Henry II and, from 1197, archdeacon of Oxford. He was a Herefordshire man and put many local legends into his collection of anecdotes. *De Nugis Curialium* ed. and trans. M. R. James: revised C. N. L. Brooke and R. A. B. Mynors, 1983.
Later stories about Eadric that were told locally have been collected by nineteenth and twentieth century folklorists, e.g. *Shropshire Folklore: A Sheaf of Gleanings* C. S. Burne 1883; *The Folklore of the Welsh Border* J. Simpson 1976.

Songs & Dances for Spring & Summer

These songs were jotted down in post-Norman times; they are 'pop' songs, showing no Norman influence either in language or mood.

(a) At a sprynge wel under a thorn
   Ther was bote of bale, a lytel here aforn:
   Ther biside stant a mayde
   Fulle of love y-bounde.
   Ho-so wol seche truwe love
   Yn hyr hyt schal be founde.

"At the source of a spring under a hawthorn tree there was a cure for sorrow (or, a remedy against harm) a little while ago. Beside them (the well and the tree) stands a young girl (or, a virgin) full of love, held fast by love. Who-ever wants to seek for true love will find it in her."

An amorous girl? A water-elf or wood-elf? Our Lady – Freo? Eostre? Mary? Any or all of them according to one's state of mind?

(b) Of *everykune tre*   (every species of tree)
   Of everykune tre
   The hawethorn *blowet suotes*   (blooms sweetest)
   Of everykune tre.

   My *lemmon* sse ssal be   (O.E. leofman – loved one, sweetheart)
   My lemmon sse ssal be
   The fairest of *erthkinne*,   (the race of earth: Mother Earth's kindred)
   My lemmon sse ssal be.

Is she a wood-elf or a girl met at a Maying?

(c) Maiden in the *mor* lay   (moor)
   In the mor lay
   Sevenight fulle –
   Sevenight fulle –
   Maiden in the mor lay
   In the mor lay
   Sevenightes fulle and a day.
   Wel was hire *mete*   (good . . . food)
   What was hire mete?
   The *primerole* and the   (primula veris 'cowslip'; is also
   The primerole and the   used for 'field daisy' in herbals)

46

Wel was hire mete.
What was hire mete?
The primerole and the violet.

Wel was hire *dring*   (drink)
(Question and answer repeated to the same pattern)

The *cheld* water of the well-spring   (chill, cold)
Wel was her *bowr*   (bower)
(Question and answer repeated to the same pattern)

The rede rose and the lilye *flour*.   (flower)

English Question:

Who is this 'maiden' who has spent a seven-night's vigil on the moor beside a well? ...a child of nature, whether human or faery, her meat the primrose and the violet, her drink the chilled water of the well-spring... The reference to a well-spring suggests the possibility that the song may originally have had some connection with the 'well-wakes' – the worship of wells – for which there is abundant evidence, went on all through the Middle Ages. These well-wakes were particularly associated with *St John's Eve* and so with the rites, ceremonies and practices of *the great Midsummer festival* as a whole. (Kathleen Herbert's italics)

(John Speirs, *Medieval English Poetry*)

Answer from Germany:

The anonymous English song of the moor-maiden must be understood in the light of the popular belief to which it alludes... What is a moor-maiden? (O.E. wylde-elfen) She is a kind of water-sprite living on the moors; she appears in a number of German legends, especially from Franconia. It is appropriate that the English song should be a dance song, as one of the commonest legends associates the moor-maiden with a dance. She tends to appear at village dances in the guise of a beautiful maiden to fascinate the young men there, but she must always return to the moor at a fixed hour or else she dies... In the English song, however, the well and the flowers evoke the moor-maiden's more-than earthly serenity and well-being: she has none of the cares or needs that mortals have.

(Peter Dronke, *The Medieval Lyric*)

The Heathen English Calendar (see pages 20-24)

Latin	Old English	Modern English
December	Ærra Geola	Going-before Yule
Winter Solstice	Geol	Yule
Nativity	Monranect*	Mothers' Night
		(New year began)
January	Æftera Geola	After Yule
February	Solmonaþ*	Mud Month
		(cf "February Filldyke")
March	Hreðmonaþ*	Hreth's Month (a goddess)
"month of Mars"		
April	Eostremonaþ*	Eostre's Month (a goddess)
May	Þrimilci	Three Milkings
June	Ærra Liða	Going-before Midsummer
Summer Solstice	Liða* (censored!)	Midsummer
July	Æftera Liða	After Midsummer
August	Weodmonaþ	Weed Month
September	Haligmonaþ*	Holy Month
	(later Hærfestmonaþ -	Harvest Month)
October	Winterfylleþ	Winter-Full-Moon
hiems plenilunio =	Wintirfillith	(the first full moon of winter)
hiems = winter		
pleni = full		
lunio = lunation		
November	Blotmonaþ*	Sacrifice Month

* = the comments of the post-Christian scholars indicate either the honouring of a divinity/divinities or a religious rite.

The Myth of Origins

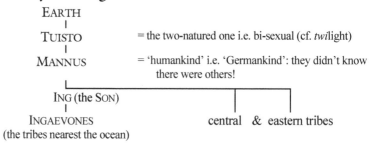

EARTH
|
TUISTO = the two-natured one i.e. bi-sexual (cf. *twi*light)
|
MANNUS = 'humankind' i.e. 'Germankind': they didn't know there were others!

ING (the SON)
|
INGAEVONES   central & eastern tribes
(the tribes nearest the ocean)

48

Glossary of Place Names

ABINGDON, Oxfordshire: shield and sheaf divination tenth century.

BARNSDALE, Yorkshire: area of waste formerly lying athwart the Roman road south of Wentbridge [Ordinance Survey SE4817]. Like SHERWOOD, it was a focus for Robin Hood ballads and stories.

BENTY GRANGE, Hartington, Derbyshire [SK1464]: primary barrow burial where boar-crest helmet was found. Now in Sheffield City Museum.

BRUNESWALD: formerly great woodland area lying between Stamford and Northampton, recalled in place-names such as Newton Bromswold [SP9966]. One of Hereward's bases.

ELY, Cambridgeshire: once an island in the Fens, held by Hereward in epic siege 1070–71.

ETON, Berkshire: Harvest Queen ritual witnessed in the sixteenth century.

FREO/FRIGU NAMES:

FREEFOLK (Frigefolc eleventh century) Whitchurch, Hants. [SU4892]

FRIDEN (Frigeden tenth century, Stanifridenmuth thirteenth century) Hartington. [SK1360]

FROYLE (Freohyll eleventh century) Winchester, Hants [SU4829]

FRYUP (Frehope, Frihopp thirteenth century) valley with beck flowing into the Esk, Yorkshire. [NZ7023–4]

GOODMANHAM (Godmundingaham eighth century) Yorkshire [SE8842]: royal temple of Deira.

GRIMSBY, Lincs. The foundation legend celebrates Anglo-Danish unity.

LYDBURY NORTH, Salop [SO3486]: in legend, Eadric the Wild was lord here; most of his manors were around Richard's Castle. [SO4969]

PETERBOROUGH, Cambs. The Wild Hunt was reported here 1127.

RENDLESHAM (Rendlesham, Mansio Rendili eighth century), Suffolk [TM3449]: royal centre of the East Anglian dynasty.

SUTTON HOO, Suffolk [TM2849]: royal cemetery of the East Anglian dynasty. Burials were conducted with various pagan rites.

THUNDERSLEY (Thunreslea eleventh century), Essex. [TQ7788]

TUESLEY (Tiwesle eleventh century), Godalming, Surrey. [SU9743]

WANSDYKE (Wodnes dic): linear earthwork in two sections, Maes Knoll to Bathampton, Somerset [ST6066–7866]; Morgan's Hill to Savernake Forest, Wiltshire. [SU0266–2166]

WARWICK: romantically explained by a monk of St Albans (thirteenth century) as *Wærmundes wic*, home of Wærmund, father of Offa I of Angeln. His legend was relocated in Mercia, kingdom of his descendant Offa II.

YEAVERING (Adgefrin eighth century), Northumberland [NT9330]: royal centre of Bernicia, with temple converted to Christian use by Paulinus.

49

An English (Anglo-Saxon) Futhorc

ᚠ	ᚢ	ᚦ	ᚩ	ᚱ	ᚳ	ᚷ	ᚹ
f	u	þ (th)	o	r	c	g	w
ᚻ	ᚾ	ᛁ	ᛄ	ᛇ	ᛈ	ᛉ	ᛋ
h	n	i	j	ih	p	x	s
ᛏ	ᛒ	ᛖ	ᛗ	ᛚ	ᛝ	ᛞ	ᛟ
t	b	e	m	l	ng	d	œ
ᚪ	ᚫ	ᛠ	ᚣ	ᛡ			
a	æ	ea	y	ia			

Maps

People and Places

SCRIDE FINNAS
[Lapps]

SWEDES

V.
U.

Götland
G

Götland
G

J

D

Bornholm
B

E

INGAEVONES

FRISIANS

Weser

SAXONS
(Seaxe)

RUGIANS

Vistula

HEATHOBARDS

VANDALS

LOMBARDS

BURGUNDIANS

X. FRANKS

Rhine

W.

Elbe

Oder

Danube

VISIGOTHS

LOMBARDS

OSTRO-
GOTHS

Vandals
to
Africa

Rome

52

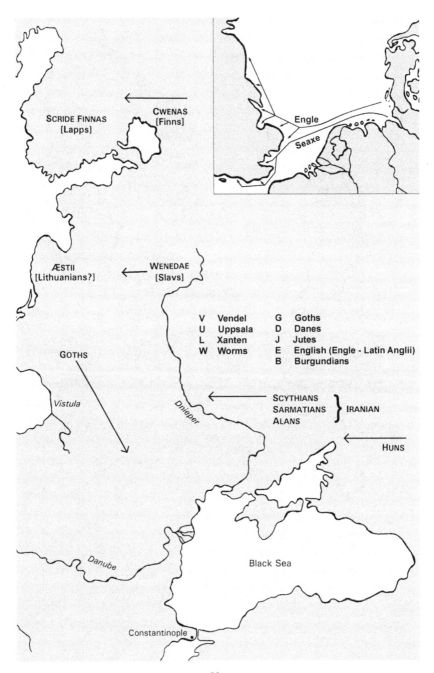

SCRIDE FINNAS
[Lapps]

CWENAS
[Finns]

Engle

Seaxe

ÆSTII
[Lithuanians?]

WENEDAE
[Slavs]

V	Vendel	G	Goths
U	Uppsala	D	Danes
L	Xanten	J	Jutes
W	Worms	E	English (Engle - Latin Anglii)
		B	Burgundians

GOTHS

Vistula

Dnieper

SCYTHIANS
SARMATIANS } IRANIAN
ALANS

HUNS

Danube

Black Sea

Constantinople

53

Poems and Stories

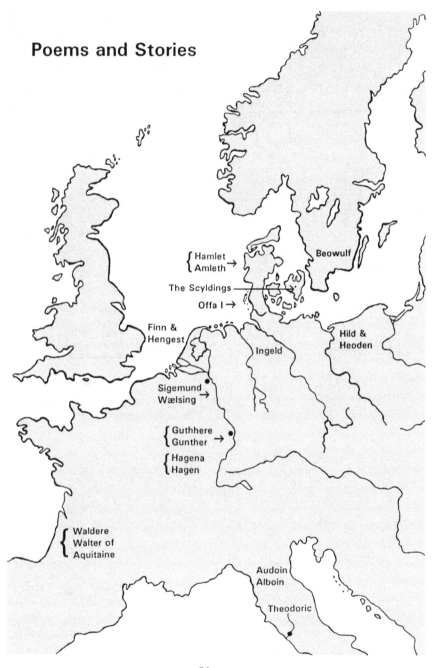

Hamlet
Amleth →

Beowulf

The Scyldings ——

Offa I →

Finn &
Hengest

Hild &
Heoden

Ingeld

Sigemund
Wælsing →

Guthhere
Gunther →

Hagena
Hagen

Waldere
Walter of
Aquitaine

Audoin
Alboin

Theodoric

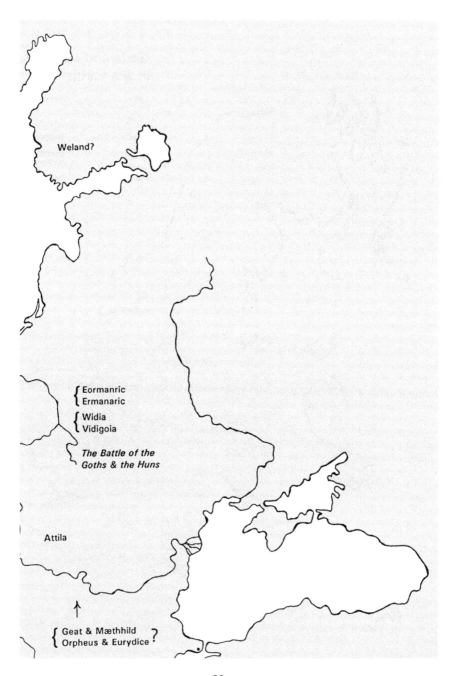

Weland?

Eormanric
Ermanaric

Widia
Vidigoia

*The Battle of the
Goths & the Huns*

Attila

Geat & Mæthhild
Orpheus & Eurydice

55

Gods and Legends in the Landscape

Offa II (combined with Offa I)	West Midlands
Havelock	Grimsby
Eadric the Wild	Shropshire
Hereward	Lincolnshire & the Fens
Robin Hood	Yorkshire & East Midlands

Yeavering

Tyne

Tees

Fryup

Goodmanham

Barnsdale
Robin Hood

Grimsby

Havelok & Goldeboru

Benty Grange

Friden

Sherwood

Trent

The Wild Hunt

Fens

Severn

Peterborough

Hereward

Lydbury North

Bruneswald

Ely

Eadric the Wild

Warwick

Rendlesham

Offa

Sutton Hoo

Fretherne

Abingdon

Thundersley

Eton

Wansdyke

Wey

Freefolk

Tuesley

Froyle

The First
England
(the land of the Engle)
at the end of 4th century

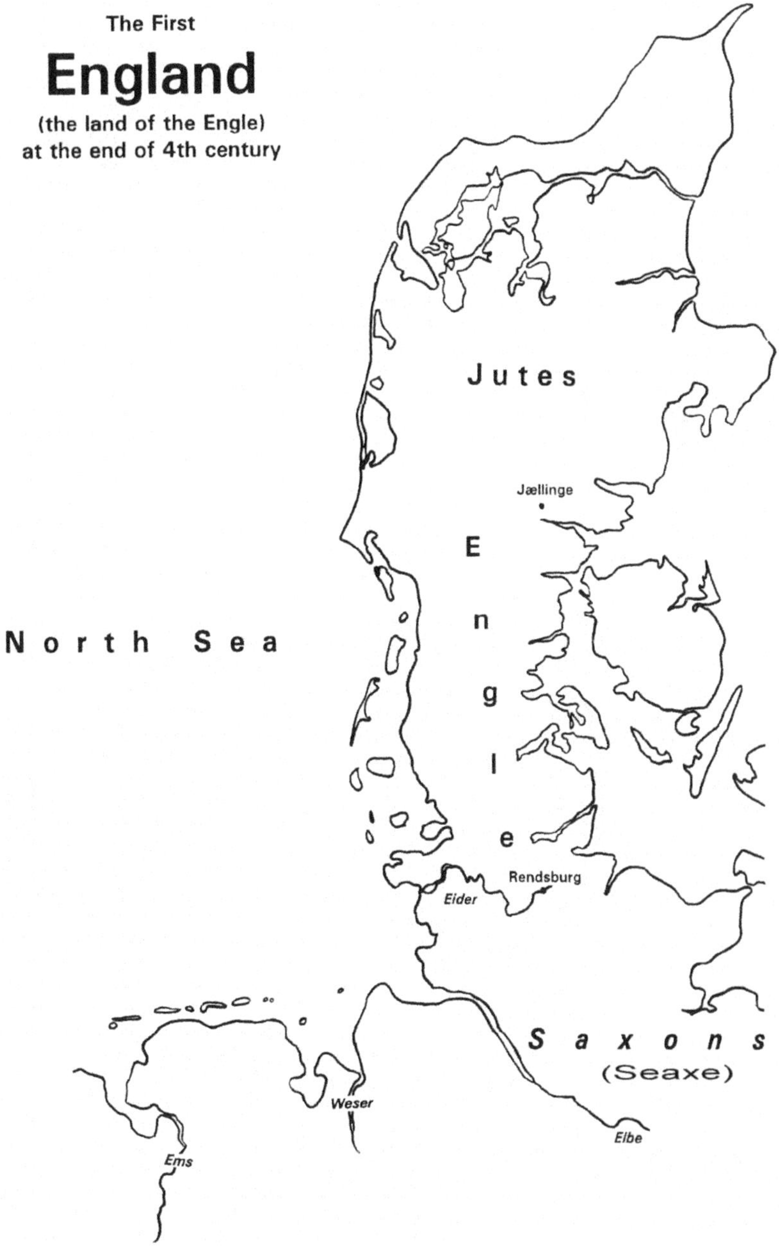

J u t e s

Jællinge
•

E

N o r t h   S e a

n

g

l

e

Rendsburg

Eider

S a x o n s
(Seaxe)

Weser

Elbe

Ems

England

Late 5th century

The West Engle were called Mercians

North
Engle

Mercians

Lindesey

East
Engle

Middle
Engle

East
Saxons

West
Saxons

Jutes

South Saxons

Jutes

58

Index

Some of our other titles

An Introduction to the Old English Language and its Literature
Stephen Pollington

The purpose of this general introduction to Old English is not to deal with the teaching of Old English but to dispel some misconceptions about the language and to give an outline of its structure and its literature. Here you will find an outline of the origins of the English language and its early literature. Such knowledge is essential to an understanding of the early period of English history and the present form of the language. This revised and expanded edition provides a useful guide for those contemplating embarking on a linguistic journey.

£5.95

First Steps in Old English
An easy to follow language course for the beginner
Stephen Pollington

A complete and easy to use Old English language course that contains all the exercises and texts needed to learn Old English. This course has been designed to be of help to a wide range of students, from those who are teaching themselves at home, to undergraduates who are learning Old English as part of their English degree course. The author has adopted a step-by-step approach that enables students of differing abilities to advance at their own pace. The course includes practice and translation exercises, a glossary of the words used in the course, and many Old English texts, including the *Battle of Brunanburh* and *Battle of Maldon*.

£16-95

Old English Poems, Prose & Lessons   2CD s
read by Stephen Pollington

This CD contains lessons and texts from *First Steps in Old English*.
Tracks include: 1. Deor. 2. Beowulf – The Funeral of Scyld Scefing. 3. Engla Tocyme (The Arrival of the English). 4. Ines Domas. Two Extracts from the Laws of King Ine. 5. Deniga Hergung (The Danes' Harrying) Anglo-Saxon Chronicle Entry AD997. 6. Durham 7. The Ordeal (Be ðon ðe ordales weddigaþ) 8. Wið Dweorh (Against a Dwarf) 9. Wið Wennum (Against Wens) 10. Wið Wæterælfadle (Against Waterelf Sickness) 11. The Nine Herbs Charm 12. Læcedomas (Leechdoms) 13. Beowulf's Greeting 14. The Battle of Brunanburh There is a Guide to Pronunciation and sixteen Reading Exercises

£15 2CDs - Free Old English transcript from www.asbooks.co.uk.

Wordcraft   Concise English/Old English Dictionary and Thesaurus
Stephen Pollington

Wordcraft provides Old English equivalents to the commoner modern words in both dictionary and thesaurus formats. The Thesaurus presents vocabulary relevant to a wide range of individual topics in alphabetical lists, thus making it easily accessible to those with specific areas of interest. Each thematic listing is encoded for cross-reference from the Dictionary.

The two sections will be of invaluable assistance to students of the language, as well as those with either a general or a specific interest in the Anglo-Saxon period.

£9.95

An Introduction to Early English Law
Bill Griffiths

Much of Anglo-Saxon life followed a traditional pattern, of custom, and of dependence on kin-groups for land, support and security. The Viking incursions of the ninth century and the re-conquest of the north that followed both disturbed this pattern and led to a new emphasis on centralised power and law, with royal and ecclesiastical officials prominent as arbitrators and settlers of disputes.

The diversity and development of early English law is sampled here by selecting several law-codes to be read in translation – that of Ethelbert of Kent, being the first to be issued in England, Alfred the Great's, the most clearly thought-out of all, and short codes from the reigns of Edmund and Ethelred the Unready.

£5.95

Peace-Weavers and Shield-Maidens: Women in Early English Society
Kathleen Herbert

The recorded history of the English people did not start in 1066 as popularly believed but one thousand years earlier. The Roman historian Cornelius Tacitus noted in *Germania*, published in the year 98, that the English (Latin *Anglii*), who lived in the southern part of the Jutland peninsula, were members of an alliance of Goddess-worshippers. The author has taken that as an appropriate opening to an account of the earliest Englishwomen, the part they played in the making of England, what they did in peace and war, the impressions they left in Britain and on the continent, how they were recorded in the chronicles, how they come alive in heroic verse and jokes.

£5.95

Dark Age Naval Power
A Reassessment of Frankish and Anglo-Saxon Seafaring Activity
John Haywood

In the first edition of this work, published in 1991, John Haywood argued that the capabilities of the pre-Viking Germanic seafarers had been greatly underestimated. Since that time, his reassessment of Frankish and Anglo-Saxon shipbuilding and seafaring has been widely praised and accepted.

'The book remains a historical study of the first order. It is required reading for our seminar on medieval seafaring at Texas A & M University and is essential reading for anyone interested in the subject.'

F. H. Van Doorninck, *The American Neptune*

'The author has done a fine job, and his clear and strongly put theories will hopefully further the discussion of this important part of European history.'

Arne Emil Christensen, *The International Journal of Nautical Archaeology*

In this second edition, some sections of the book have been revised and updated to include information gained from excavations and sea trials with sailing replicas of early ships. The new evidence supports the author's argument that early Germanic shipbuilding and seafaring skills were far more advanced than previously thought. It also supports the view that Viking ships and seaborne activities were not as revolutionary as is commonly believed.

5 maps & 18 illustrations

£18.95 hardback

The Rebirth of England and English: The Vision of William Barnes

Fr. Andrew Phillips

English history is patterned with spirits so bright that they broke through convention and saw another England. Such was the case of the Dorset poet, William Barnes (1801–86), priest, poet, teacher, self-taught polymath, linguist extraordinary and that rare thing – a man of vision. In this work the author looks at that vision, a vision at once of Religion, Nature, Art, Marriage, Society, Economics, Politics and Language. He writes: 'In search of authentic English roots and values, our post-industrial society may well have much to learn from Barnes'.

For the first time Saxon-English words created and used by Barnes have been gathered together and listed next to their foreign equivalents.

£6.95

English Heroic Legends

Kathleen Herbert

The author has taken the skeletons of ancient Germanic legends about great kings, queens and heroes, and put flesh on them. Kathleen Herbert's encyclopaedic knowledge of the period is reflected in the wealth of detail she brings to these tales of adventure, passion, bloodshed and magic.

The book is in two parts. First are the stories that originate deep in the past, yet because they have not been hackneyed they are still strange and enchanting. After that there is a selection of the source material, with information about where it can be found and some discussion about how it can be used. The purpose of the work is to bring pleasure to those studying Old English literature and, more importantly, to bring to the attention of a wider public the wealth of material that has yet to be tapped by modern writers, composers and artists.

Kathleen Herbert is the author of a trilogy, set in sixth century Britain, which includes a winner of the Georgette Heyer prize for an outstanding historical novel.

£9.95

The Anglo-Saxon Monastic Sign Language

Monasteriales Indicia

Edited with notes and translation by Debby Banham

The *Monasteriales Indicia* is one of very few texts which let us see how life was really lived in monasteries in the early Middle Ages. Written in Old English and preserved in a manuscript of the mid-eleventh century, it consists of 127 signs used by Anglo-Saxon monks during the times when the Benedictine Rule forbade them to speak. These indicate the foods the monks ate, the clothes they wore, and the books they used in church and chapter, as well as the tools they used in their daily life, and persons they might meet both in the monastery and outside. The text is printed here with a parallel translation. The introduction gives a summary of the background, both historical and textual, as well as a brief look at the later evidence for monastic sign language in England. Extensive notes provide the reader with details of textual relationships, explore problems of interpretation, and set out the historical implications of the text.

£6.95

Anglo-Saxon FAQs
Stephen Pollington
125 questions and answers on a wide range of topics.
Are there any Anglo-Saxon jokes? Who was the Venerable Bede? Did the women wear make-up? What musical instruments did they have? How was food preserved? Did they have shops? Did their ships have sails? Why was Ethelred called 'Unready'? Did they have clocks? Did they celebrate Christmas? What are runes? What weapons and tactics did they use? Were there female warriors? What was the Synod of Whitby?

£9.95

Aspects of Anglo-Saxon Magic
Bill Griffiths
Magic is something special, something unauthorised; an alternative perhaps; even a deliberate cultivation of dark, evil powers. But for the Anglo-Saxon age, the neat division between mainstream and occult, rational and superstitious, Christian and pagan is not always easy to discern. To maintain its authority (or its monopoly?) the Church drew a formal line and outlawed a range of dubious practices (like divination, spells, folk healing) while at the same time conducting very similar rituals itself, and may even have adapted legends of elves to serve in a Christian explanation of disease as a battle between good and evil, between Church and demons; in other cases powerful ancestors came to serve as saints.

In pursuit of a better understanding of Anglo-Saxon magic, a wide range of topics and texts are examined in this book, challenging (constructively, it is hoped) our stereotyped images of the past and its beliefs.

Texts are printed in their original language (e.g. Old English, Icelandic, Latin) with New English translations. Contents include:– twenty charms; the English, Icelandic and Norwegian rune poems; texts on dreams, weather signs, unlucky days, the solar system; and much more.

£16.95   hardback

Anglo-Saxon Runes
John M. Kemble
Kemble's essay *On Anglo-Saxon Runes* first appeared in the journal *Archaeologia* for 1840; it draws on the work of Wilhelm Grimm, but breaks new ground for Anglo-Saxon studies in his survey of the Ruthwell Cross and the Cynewulf poems. It is an expression both of his own indomitable spirit and of the fascination and mystery of the Runes themselves, making it an attractive introduction to the topic.
For this edition new notes have been supplied, which include translations of Latin and Old English material quoted in the text, to make this key work in the study of runes more accessible to the general reader.

£5.95

Organisations

Þa Engliscan Gesiðas

Þa Engliscan Gesiðas (The English Companions) is a historical and cultural society exclusively devoted to Anglo-Saxon history. Its aims are to bridge the gap between scholars and non-experts, and to bring together all those with an interest in the Anglo-Saxon period, its language, culture and traditions. The Fellowship publishes a journal, *Wiðowind*. For further details see www.tha-engliscan-gesithas.org.uk or write to: Membership Secretary, The English Companions, PO Box 62790, London, SW12 2BH, England, UK

Regia Anglorum

Our aim is to portray as accurately as possible the life and times of the people who lived in the British Isles around a thousand years ago. We investigate a wide range of crafts and have a Living History Exhibit that frequently erects some thirty tented period structures. We have a large Anglo-Saxon hall and six full scale period boats ranging from 6 metre to 15 metres. Regia Anglorum has a thriving membership and 40 branches in the British Isles and United States - so there might be one near you. We especially welcome families with children. www.regia.org   *General information* eolder@regia.org   *Membership* join@regia.org

The Sutton Hoo Society

Our aims and objectives focus on promoting research and education relating to the Anglo-Saxon Royal cemetery at Sutton Hoo, Suffolk in the UK. The Society publishes a newsletter SAXON twice a year. For information about membership see website: www.suttonhoo.org

Wuffing Education

Wuffing Education provides those interested in the history, archaeology, literature and culture of the Anglo-Saxons with the chance to meet experts and fellow enthusiasts for a whole day of in-depth seminars and discussions. Day Schools at Tranmer House, Sutton Hoo, Suffolk. Wuffing Education, 4 Hilly Fields, Woodbridge, Suffolk IP12 4DX, England education@wuffings.co.uk   web www.wuffings.co.uk   Tel. 01394 383908 or 01728 688749

Places to visit

Bede's World at Jarrow

Bede's world tells the remarkable story of the life and times of the Venerable Bede. Bede's World, Church Bank, Jarrow, Tyne and Wear, NE32 3DY Tel. 0191 489 2106; Fax: 0191 428 2361; website: www.bedesworld.co.uk

Sutton Hoo near Woodbridge, Suffolk

Sutton Hoo is a group of low burial mounds. Excavations in 1939 brought to light the richest burial ever discovered in Britain. Some original objects as well as replicas of the treasure are on display. National Trust - 2 miles east of Woodbridge on B1083   Tel. 01394 389700

West Stow Anglo-Saxon Village

An early Anglo-Saxon Settlement reconstructed on the site where it was excavated consisting of timber and thatch hall, houses and workshop. There is also a museum containing objects found during the excavation of the site. For details see www.weststow.org or contact: The Visitor Centre, West Stow Country Park, Icklingham Road, West Stow, Bury St Edmunds, Suffolk IP28 6HG   Tel. 01284 728718

Lightning Source UK Ltd.
Milton Keynes UK
UKHW022024220922
409278UK00006B/1379